Publish and be damned
www.pabd.com

The Escapist

James Morris

Publish and be damned
www.pabd.com

First published in Great Britain 2005 by James Morris.
The moral right of James Morris to be identified as the author of this work has been asserted.

Designed in London, Great Britain, by Adlibbed Limited.
Printed and bound in the UK or the US.

ISBN: 1-905290-05-5

This book is a work of fiction.

For my family, but especially Flora, William and Haydn, who make words seem so empty, even finely crafted ones.

Log 000000000001 – I think therefore I am, therefore I act.

They arrested the code dudes in an operation sweeping the entire city. My Pocket Assistant beeped impetuously as Rodriguez dialled the tip-off pager number. Something heavy was going down. Nobody used those digits unless it was a dire emergency. I flipped the cover off the Phoenix handheld and studied the holographic touch screen. The message flashed across in chiselled 3D text:

Pigs can fly, and they're flying right into our roost. There ain't nobody here but us chickens...

I found a secluded spot in the changing room of Selfridges on Oxford Street, spoke the security code into my pocket computer, and hit erase. All my once valuable Intel account numbers, now useless and incriminating, disappeared off to digital nirvana, shredded according to American Federal standards and then scrambled still further by encryption software I'd bought from a Bosnian hacker for half a million Euros. I was clean. If somebody came after me during the crackdown, there wouldn't be any evidence that my diversion of American hedge funds to non-existent bank accounts had anything to do with me. No more of that stolen Yankee money for my pocket, at least not for a while. But there was a bright side. I wouldn't be spending any time in penal stasis, like the majority of London's vast hacker population.

Leaving the changing room, I handed the glitter suit I'd been pretending to try on back to the attendant and returned to the clothing racks. Despite the convenience of holographic on-line shopping, there was still something enticing about seeing all the latest clothing styles side by side on their hangers. Real shopping was never going to die, unlike real fucking. Lightweight strap-ons had become remarkably affordable and easy to use. Many people had decided that pleasuring themselves was far more satisfying than having to deal with the annoyances of actual people. Singles bars had become rare, and pornography even more profitable. But shopping was different. I loved searching for the latest attire in a physical shop. You never knew what you wanted until you found it, and the quest was almost more fun than the purchase. It was expensive, but I'd always had the extra money it cost to shop in person.

At least, I had done until a few minutes previously. I was at a loss. My most lucrative ever vein of fraudulence had reached an abrupt end. I had to find another scam, but I also needed to lie low. The easiest place to hide from police is right under their noses. That was why I got involved with COSI - the Central Office for Strategic Intelligence, and the very organisation that had captured most of my criminal colleagues.

I'd heard about the new spate of Mind Invasions from the news bulletin my Home Information System retrieved for me daily. That was, the one day a week I bothered to read the fabricated garbage the culture industry fed into Infonet. The bulletin reported how famous scientists recently returned from cryogenic sabbatical were being kidnapped and their minds drained of useful information. They were then left as vegetables, their consciousnesses irretrievably submerged in the noodle soup which was all that was left of their brains. After a bit of research into related vacancies, I'd applied for a job with COSI searching the neural highways of these unfortunate victims for clues. My fake qualifications in psychology and neurolectric interfaces, plus a natural talent for verbal diarrhoea, easily landed me the post. I started immediately. It was good cover, particularly as the job meant I could pretend to be a hot-shot neuro-psychologist. Nobody understood what it was I did, including me, but everyone agreed it was important. I also hoped that whoever was doing these Invasions would approach me to become a partner. It looked like a lucrative business, and I wanted in after the Intel Fund fiasco.

My first research subject was Eric von Kühnert. Before his kidnapping, he had been a fibre-optics expert on loan from Siemens to the postal service. He was a loner, with a taste for topless-bottomless bars. During a night hopping from bar to bar he'd been caught by the mind invaders. They'd picked him up when he was concentrating on one of the artificially-structured beauties at Pee Wee's Strontium Gold, an establishment that specialised in girls just over the legal age, although many were probably under. His favourite drink, fittingly entitled a Kesey Cool-Aid Special, had been laced with that age-old perennial LSD while neither he nor his musclebound bodyguards were paying attention. As a result he'd had very little hold on reality when they came to get him. They'd easily disposed of the bodyguards. These two had been found a week afterwards, decapitated and naked in the deep freeze of a local French Restaurant.

Large traces of the LSD were still in the scientist's bloodstream when he turned up at his apartment a few days later. Nobody was really sure how he'd made it into the heavily-guarded South Kensington mansion building without anyone noticing. But he'd been there for over a day when they discovered him, sitting calmly in a leather armchair.

***

There was something very strange about von Kühnert's blank psyche, but I couldn't put my finger on it. Nosing around with the VR rig in the empty corridors of his mind, I could find nothing personal about him at all. The standard rig I was using reminded me of the remote control sets I'd operated when I was serving in the European Rapid Response Air Force. I had shot down two U.S. F-55s over Portugal without leaving a bunker in Hertfordshire. What a stupid war - six days long, with only thirty casualties (most of them from friendly fire) and nothing proven. Europe, with the newly-enlisted Ukraine, was an easy military equal of America. There was no point in any kind of competition between them except through trade. But even legitimate international commerce had become a stalemate, the major markets being so well protected by import taxation. The true battle was being waged by the underground businessmen such as myself, acting illegally in any country we chose. Many of us worked for the big corporations directly, although no company would admit it. That was how the most important goods moved across international boundaries, and how economic advantages were taken by one country over another.

The inner highways of von Kühnert's strangely absent mind were like the empty tunnels of New York's disused subway – dark, dirty and dreamlike. I was using the VR rig's Hypermove function to speed my way through these tunnels while the plan of this neural maze was recorded on the flash memory of the Philips T1000. I intended to take a closer look at the schematic later. Instead of organised search, I was randomly hunting around to see if there was anything there. All I found was empty space. According to the scientific paper I'd skim-read the night before, with this kind of search you'd normally come up against all kinds of personifications of the subject's thought processes. It wouldn't be so easy to move around. You'd draw to a halt in a few virtual metres, unless the subject was unusually open and didn't mind giving out personal information, which nobody really was. Von Kühnert was totally devoid of anything, yet he wasn't dead. If he had been, there wouldn't have been any structures to see at all – merely swirling polygons like those produced by early VR systems. This kind of random geometry was the end product of a graphics mapping system with nothing to map. I once logged into a guy's mind during the last four minutes of his life after I'd shot him, for kicks. It's hard to describe the scenes I witnessed - certainly nothing like the media cliché of green fields and sky. What I saw was due to the system having less and less to lock onto as the brain activity of the dying person faded. The distinct pictures that were conjured up, mostly evil-looking naked hermaphrodites, blurred into multicoloured polygons in eerie ways, then fizzled out. It was a sight far more beautiful than the Aurora Borealis, and far less expensive than a trip to Scandinavia. I don't even remember what this particular person's name was. Life had become pretty cheap, unlike information. He'd meant to forcibly obtain some facts worth rather a lot to an international pop music bulletin. Instead he'd had his vital internal organs splattered all over an adjacent wall.

COSI was an interesting place to work, especially as it was the Establishment, or what was left of it. Most of world government had been replaced by the infrastructure of multinationals. All that was left were police forces and the penal system, and even they were biased towards the people who donated large quantities to law-enforcement funding bodies. So, in reality, I was working for organised industry. It was more like being a private investigator than a forensic cop, not that I really had any qualifications to be either. I was reporting directly to Vanessa Carmichael, COSI's director of digital investigations. She was an incredibly tough and resourceful woman.

Carmichael had landed the top job after her predecessor was removed in a wave of adverse publicity. It was a typically British scandal. Apparently he'd been using his position of power to extort sexual favours from up-and-coming hopefuls, male and female. In exchange for bizarre acts of perversion, he offered a healthy career path. He'd tried this with one very promising young lady and she'd threatened to expose him. Similar situations had happened to him countless times, but he was such a pro at the espionage and enforcement business that he either knew something about his accusers to shut them up, or he had them quietly killed. But this particular lady had been too smart for him. She was totally clean, beyond blackmail, and had efficiently dealt with every assassination agent sent. She knew when each one was coming and somehow headed them off with blackmail of her own. Eventually COSI's director of digital investigations had to step down in a hail of controversy. The woman did well after the incident. She was none other than Vanessa Carmichael herself, his successor.

I didn't want to cross someone with that kind of reputation. Nevertheless, I was surprised that a law-enforcement professional so respected and feared among the criminal community should fail to notice my shady identity. I didn't have any convictions and I'd never been explicitly implicated in any of the collapsed illegalities with which I'd been involved. But I expected that such a paragon of investigation would have some information about me which even I didn't know existed. If she did, it hadn't stopped her signing me up. Maybe it even improved my job prospects – it takes a thief to catch a thief and all that.

I entered Carmichael's office for the first time to report on my initial trip into von Kühnert's cerebrum.

"Sit down", she ordered before I'd even finished walking through the door. She looked only slightly older than me, but her voice had an imperative quality mine could only partially make up for in charm and seduction. I sat down in a comfortable cloned-leather chair - still an expensive item, despite the new cloning expansion slots for the latest pocket computers. Carmichael looked at me with a thoroughly undecipherable expression. She was strangely attractive, for a slightly plump woman perilously closing in on middle age. After a time, during which I felt like I was being given a full-body X-ray and sonogram, she spoke:

"Well, Mr Dean, what have you got for me today?" was all she said. And then the first sign of any emotion: her lips curled upwards slightly at the edges, in what must have been a vain attempt at a smile. It looked more like a symmetrical facial tic in slow motion.

"He's totally wiped, Vanessa," I began. "I don't know why they didn't just kill the poor vegetable off."

Carmichael nodded. She looked a little bemused by my use of her first name. "Memory is just biological disk space. Data is never fully wiped for someone who knows how it has been shredded," she proposed.

"And that's the big problem," I continued. "We have to find the specific way his mind has been erased after they got what they wanted out of him. What exactly was he working on when he was abducted?"

"I'll get Industrial Intelligence to put something together for you. It'll be on your home system when you get there this evening. You can study it tonight." I nodded sagely, and then there was a silence of a good many seconds.

"Any chance of a drink?" I ventured, in an attempt to loosen up the atmosphere. There was a further pause in the proceedings as Carmichael had her secretary, an extremely effeminate dwarf of a man, fetch me a coffee-flavoured mineral water. When this had arrived and I'd taken a few sips I outlined my plan of action. "Look, Vanessa, I need to make a study. I know what it's like inside a dead person's mind, but I want to compare this scientist's blank brain with the insides of naturally intellectually-challenged minds. I think the differences between the two could give me a clue as to exactly where amongst his empty passages the ghost of von Kühnert's consciousness lives. I want to go to the Nexus-7 Neurological Institute with clearance to venture inside a few of their permanent holidaymakers."

Nexus-7 was the leading hospital for chronic mental illness, situated on the Moon. All the most incurable psychopaths and prematurely senile people were sent there, either by their loved ones or private police forces like COSI. I didn't really want to go to Nexus-7, but it would be a good excuse to enjoy the Moon's famously debauched nightlife. It would also give me time away from direct COSI surveillance, just in case someone with a more lucrative offer wanted to get in contact.

"You're quite a harsh little man, aren't you?" interjected Carmichael with surprising acidity. "A typical scientist." For a moment I thought she could hear what I was thinking. I frowned and rejoined, "I beg your pardon?" There was another weighty silence while I surveyed her and she stared at me with that unreadable impassive face of hers. I wondered again what she knew about my true background. Then suddenly the uncomfortable moment was over.

"Of course, every avenue will be laid open to you without question," said Carmichael. The mood had changed in a very random way as if her previous comment had never existed. I was unusually perturbed. I could manipulate most people, particularly women, but working out what was going on in Carmichael's mind was beyond me. I concluded with resignation that she was probably smarter than I was - not something I was used to. "Would you be ready to travel tomorrow?" She continued. I nodded, still frowning. Carmichael rose from her chair and I was slightly diverted by the swing of her hips, which seemed out of place. Something about her made me think of a severe old matron in the body of an expensive holographic porn queen, or maybe vice versa. She rested herself on the edge of the desk in front of me and fixed her eyes on mine with total confidence. "This Mind Invasion business is beginning to be a bit of a problem to our industrial friends. Rounding up all the hackers hasn't helped. It's fundamentally important that we sort the situation out as soon as possible. It's also very much in your personal interest. I do hope you understand."

Log 000000000101 - Knowledge is power in the information age. The more you know, the easier it is to gain control over other people, and whoever has the greatest access to information wins.

On the shuttle to Nexus-7 I mulled over the report from Industrial Intelligence. Von Kühnert's area of expertise didn't bear any direct relation to what other Mind Invasion victims had been concerned with. All of the scientists were in different fields, but all of them were considered leading experts. I reckoned there had to be a connection between the cryogenic sabbaticals and each kidnap. But this obvious link had been checked and rechecked by other COSI operatives to no avail. The cryogenic parlour owners had been interrogated thoroughly using the latest cranial X-rays, and every single one had truthfully denied involvement. After some rather fruitless pondering, I wondered how I would be able to turn this situation to my advantage with Carmichael around. It was unusual for me to come across somebody so unreadable. She was legendary, but then so was I, albeit always as an untraceable alias.

Despite my many trips around the Solar System, it still filled me with joy to leave Earth. I loved the planetary views in transit, and I adored the notion that mankind was no longer tied to an arbitrary hunk of minerals, and was instead in a position to choose between a selection of hunks of minerals to live on. But most of all, my excitement arose simply from travelling itself. I got a childish kick out of being in any kind of vehicle, particularly one going somewhere fast. Moving from A to B felt like what life itself was all about. Getting there was always an anticlimax.

The Moon looked eerie in the darkness as we crossed from the shuttle pad. A guy called Chucky, one of COSI's minor moon operatives, picked me up from the pad in a small but comfortably pressurised balloon-wheeled vehicle. He was outrageously fat, but he lived on the Moon most of the time so it didn't matter too much. The journey was fairly short, which was fortunate as Chucky was annoyingly nerdish. He wouldn't stop making inane factual comments about our moon transport, despite my complete lack of verbal response to his monologue. I may have been tempted to torture and kill him had we been stuck for any extended period of time together. That would not have been the most effective COSI career move, but it would have had the advantage of being highly satisfying.

Nexus-7 was one of the cleanest places I'd ever seen, considering that dust got everywhere on the Moon. If you imagined a North African desert with the area of about two North Americas, then took away the air and the Arabs, you'd get the picture. How they kept the dust out of the colonies there was just another miracle of contemporary science. The Nexus-7 rest colony for human vegetables was in a league of its own, however. It felt like the most ordered place I'd ever been to. Even the notice boards had identically-sized notes pinned to them in perfect grid arrays, with no missing spots. I wondered if you had to wait for a vacancy to put up a note, and couldn't take one down until a replacement was found. Trying my best to walk in perfectly equal steps so as not to break the Nexus-7 symmetry, I followed Chucky's chubby form through the pristine hallways. He was taking me to meet the head of patient care. As I walked about the facility observing the staff I began to realise that everyone here was overweight in some way or another. Everyone had been genetically and surgically in perfect shape inside the Moon resorts I'd visited before, particularly in the leisure developments around the new space port. The permanent lunar residents not so intent on making an exhibition of themselves obviously let the very low gravity do its work. Here they could get heavier without a negative effect on mobility. Some of them were so rotund you could have used them as wheels on their own lunar transportation vehicles. I'd never realised before that the Moon was a regular haven for the mass disadvantaged, but I supposed it all made sense.

After introducing myself to Nexus-7's chief medical consultant, I explained my need to use a VR rig to analyse the effects of memory loss. My research, I argued, was part of a very important piece of psychological research into aphasia - my official cover, created for me by COSI. Without needing to go into too much detail, I was escorted to the main ward. My guide was a portly but passable nurse called Sophie. I set the equipment up in an empty private room and Sophie brought in a few of the memory-loss patients in succession. Each one was different inside. I recorded the sessions on the Philips T1000's hard storage to look at later if I needed to refresh my own memory. None of these minds were as bare as von Kühnert's. Their mental passageways were not so well-defined, either. Many of the brains I explored had corridors that narrowed so as to be impassable, while others cut off and brought you back in impossible loops that were different each time you traversed them. This pointed to continuing neural subsidence.

Sophie the nurse seemed very interested in what I was doing. She said she was hoping to be a genetico-neurologist and was doing her internship here as part of a course at the Moon's Institute of Biotechnology, which was considered by many to be a refuge for dumb rich kids. I hinted that I would be perfectly happy to discuss my work with her after I'd finished my tests. That didn't take long, as I was finding my research very inconclusive, and I didn't really care that much anyway. Once the equipment was packed away I had no trouble in removing all of Sophie's clothes. Nurses always managed to live up to their reputation, at least when I was around. It was as she was riding me, in obvious ecstasy while I lay beneath her making gentle ironic thrusts, that Chucky burst in with a rapid fire handgun. I laughed out loud. He looked like an angry beach ball. With an enormous shove of my arms I launched Sophie from my lap towards him, just as she was reaching a pinnacle of joy. Chucky released a barrage of shots, all of which ripped through Sophie's body and missed me entirely. At least she died happy. Her parents wouldn't have to pay her exorbitant university fees anymore, either. They might even thank me. Chucky fell backwards from the momentum of Sophie's corpse flying toward him in the low gravity, giving me plenty of time to pull my gun, which was loaded with explosive shells, from under my nearby shirt. I blew off his right arm, the one which held his weapon. He screamed as the blood pumped out of him in spumes. I walked over to where he now lay on the ground, both my gun and my still full erection jutting out menacingly. I wondered which was the most scary to him. The notion of making him talk under the threat of perverse sexual acts danced amusingly across my mind to be discarded very rapidly. From time to time my wicked imagination revolted even myself. I pointed the gun at his head and dragged the tangled mass of him and the nurse into the room, then re-closed the door.

"Ahhhh, please don't kill me", blubbered Chucky, holding up his remaining hand as if it could provide some kind of protection.

"I may not kill you", I answered, lying. "But it would help if you tell me why COSI is trying to kill *me* before I permanently rid you of your weight problem."

I had to make some decisions fast. There was a dead student nurse and a gravely injured COSI employee lying on the floor and this would be hard to explain away as an accident. Who wanted me dead? It was unlikely to be COSI. I figured this could have been my first contact with the organisation behind the Mind Invasion kidnaps. The other hospital staff would be outside the door very soon, and the chances were they would find this situation a little odd for a research neuropsychologist. Chucky's gun was silenced, but mine had made a big noise, and a larger mess.

Chucky grimaced with pain and tried to speak again. "Not COSI...", he whimpered, and passed out. I reached down and took the security card for the moon vehicle from Chucky's breast pocket where I'd seen him put it earlier. His severed arm still held his gun. I decided not to pick it up. I forced my gun into Sophie's hand and blew Chucky's brains out. A quick fumble undid his trousers and I pulled out his scrawny male appendage. That would keep them guessing, at least until their security group arrived. It took a minute to get dressed and collect up my equipment, some of which had a few dubious flecks of blood to incriminate me. There wasn't much point in trying to cover anything up, anyway. It would take a brain scarcely larger than a baby Chihuahua's to work out that what had really been going on was not a suicidal love session between two fat people. For one thing, student nurses didn't usually carry explosive flechette handguns, except perhaps when they believed very strongly in euthanasia.

What a mess. My first comparatively honest job in years and it seemed like it was over already. I hadn't expected this kind of contact so soon. I slipped out of the Nexus-7 clinic as quickly as possible and into the late Chucky's balloon-tired moon vehicle, a piezoelectric craft made by Siemens that was powered by a bio-gravitational process. The Siemens was fun to drive, because the moon's low g's and the vehicle's large carbon-fibre tyres made an accident almost impossible. I could fling the vehicle about like a Thai jet scooter taxi but without the fear of injury. Tuning the radio transponder to a Sri-Lankan station playing loud neuro-spunk, I had an exhilaratingly bouncy ride across the dunes to Armstrong, the Moon's largest city. Then I took a magneto-bus to Buzztown, the once prestigious and expensive residential area near the old spacepad. Real estate investors had made the now classic mistake of thinking that people would commute to work from a home in a neighbourhood where nothing ever happened. They'd had to sell the buildings off for far less than expected. Since then the development had become somewhat seedy and a law unto itself. Perhaps now that there was some life there, people could be persuaded to leave Earth. But investors had given up totally in disgust and cut their losses by selling out to any shady buyer with the money up front.

Buzztown was well constructed, so the dust was in general kept out. But the atmosphere had become a bit smelly, because the climate control equipment was badly maintained. The whole moral atmosphere was rank, too. You could get some really sickening VR chips here with tongue-in-cheek titles like "Make Love To

Me and Tear Off My Limbs, I'm Swedish". You knew the title wasn't an exaggeration of the content, either. If you were truly obsessed and had a lot of money you could re-enact the simulation for real with the specially-grown clone-bot of your choice. Sixteen storeys underground I found my favourite hangout, Dirty Sara's. A potent glass of TechnoJuice in front of me, I commanded my PDA to retrieve the Moon's latest local news items. There was nothing about a vicious dual murder at Nexus-7. Carefully disguising my call-sign via an anonymous Maori re-router in New Zealand, I surfed the COSI network and scoured the files of a few key intelligence employees, including myself. I did not come up as under surveillance. I was not registered as missing. In fact, I had apparently made a report only three minutes previously about similarities between cases of Reagan's Aphasia and the problems encountered with von Kühnert. I sat back in my floating bar-chair and finished off my drink, wondering who my benevolent angel could be.

I was halfway through my second Juice when I was approached by the waiter, dressed in a pink parody of a Moulin Rouge outfit. Dirty Sara liked to indulge in sexual social comment with her staff. The waiter had a message for me. A gentleman only described as "Harry" wanted me to meet him for dinner in a few hours time in the restaurant, Dirty Sara's Quick'n'Easy. Perhaps this was the contact I was after. Perhaps they wanted to make a deal. Or perhaps it was going to be another half-hearted attempt on my life. Either way, I felt man enough to handle the situation. I told the waiter to bring me the bill and to tell Harry that I would meet him at 20:30.

I spent the three hours before the meeting getting organised. I took a room under a pseudonym at a quiet and unassuming hotel, had a shower, and ordered from room-service a replacement weapon that would fit my remaining explosive rounds. Fully kitted-out and fresh, I took the lift back to Dirty Sara's and entered the eatery. I was early, so I ordered a drink. This time I had a whiskey and cranberry juice. The menu looked good, so I chose the honeyed zero-g turbot with au gratin sweet apple-potatoes. These were a genetic hybrid of fruit and root vegetable combined into something called a froot – sweet and crunchy yet full of carbohydrates. Dirty Sara's diner had a relaxing environment, with early space scenes adorning the walls and waiters wearing bottomless costumes, another social comment. Ambient Vietnamese pop music was playing throughout the restaurant, though it was possible to change the audio for specific tables on request.

Harry arrived. He looked Southeast Asian, which was later confirmed when I learned he was from the Thai Free State. He was accompanied by a girl with the most amazing pair of legs but a face like a lamb's kidney. She was also Thai and went by the name of Santada. Harry approached with a huge grin which hardly left his face the whole time we were conversing. His associate was completely silent, but her eyes told me she knew exactly what was going on. Over dinner I learned that Harry was neither from COSI nor the group behind Chucky, whatever that was.

"My organisation does not want you dead, Mr Dean. On the contrary. We are most interested in assisting your research. We have a proposition to make to you. Your little police force would be very gratified to find out why great research scientists are losing their minds. There are also many in America who would like to find out how this has happened and what has been taken, and what for. My organisation can help you find some answers. We know that you in particular will be able to help us get what we want in return." Harry sat back and grinned an even wider, perfectly-arrayed dental display.

"What is it you want?" I asked.

"We know that you are not quite what you appear to your organisation. We have helped you out of a recent mishap at the Nexus-7 Research Centre. But we could easily place you in far greater trouble." This seemed like a combination of a threat and avoiding the question. It was yet another example of Pacific Rim inscrutability, I concluded.

"So, what do you want?" I asked again.

Harry then launched into a long and enlightening speech about von Kühnert's research and the importance of fibre-optics and neural nets. Finally, after a manufacturer's manual of technical detail, a lot of which I only vaguely understood, Harry began talking about a new kind of machine. The mind invasions were all linked to it, and Harry wanted it desperately. This was the first time I heard about Project Pure Light Abacus.

Log 000001010010 – Binary computing systems mimic the structural oppositions of human logic, and were developed from theories of language early in the 20th century. If a person is made up of memories stored in language, then an entire personality can be stored and transmitted using binary systems.

Freida was a real bimbo. Seeing her short skirt and obvious lack of wholesome underwear, most people who had ever met her quickly ascertained that she shaved all over except her head. Maybe even her luscious wavy hair was scalp-incorporated manmade fibre. It had felt real the last time I'd met her, but I hadn't seen her in years. Our previous encounter was in Prague where we'd both been trying to rob the same Russian bank. I'd had to knock her unconscious with a dead security guard's night stick to take the money for myself. It was a sensible move as she wasn't known as the Bobbitt Queen without reason. She wouldn't have let met get away with the cash otherwise. The last place I was expecting to meet her was on a shuttle back from the Moon to Earth. I learned later that it was nothing to do with coincidence. As she bent over me her cheap-looking cleavage, which had been surgically enhanced to comic proportions, jiggled into my face. Her special scent chemically engineered for her by Libyans wafted cloyingly towards my nostrils.

"Well, if it isn't my little truncheon. I hope you spent that money wisely," she purred.

There was no way she was going to start something in this closed environment, but it still couldn't be called the best of situations. I enquired if she would care to join me at the bar for drinks and left my aisle seat to follow her aft. I tried not to smile as I sensed a myriad male eyes following her aft with me. She was wearing a dress made of a material that had a sheen like silk but fitted tightly like rubber. It was green. Today her hair was blonde. She carried no bag, so unless she had a weapon concealed in one of her breasts she was not armed.

We sat at the bar.

"Your round," said Freida. "You owe me 96 million Stolis, so let's start drinking right away."

"You look well," I countered, as the barman prepared a Stoli on the rocks and a whiskey and cranberry. Freida smiled like a pubescent Lolita, except she was probably five times the right age. She was a miracle of contemporary surgery.

"And you look fantastic!" she returned, affecting coyness with a gently coquettish flick of the head.

"So what is it you want?" I asked, tired already of these verbal games. Flirtatious banter was Freida's hallmark. She'd made quite a success of what amounted to annoying people into letting their guards down.

"I hear you're going straight on some research job," she finally answered. "Word gets around. It sounds interesting. Tell me about it."

So I outlined, at very great and boring length, how I was doing research into mental illness amongst private security staff on the job. I explained how I'd been to Nexus-7 to interview some former guards and an investigator who had gone completely insane. Her attempts to get a word in and prevent this clearly erroneous tide of verbal diarrhoea were to no avail. I was finally interrupted by the call to return to our seats for re-entry into the Earth's atmosphere and landing. I apologised for the premature interruption and promised to finish the story some time later.

We landed in the City Spaceport where St. Paul's Cathedral used to be. As I left the craft Freida scurried towards me and I found it impossible to rid myself of her. After a brief walk we found ourselves at an exclusive duty-free stand selling real fruit and vegetables. The tax on legumes was becoming extortionate. I decided that I'd had enough of Freida. Choosing a sizeable courgette from the selection on show, as if to examine it, I inched towards her. With a gesture from my free hand, I remarked how wonderfully ripe the microclimate-grown star fruit looked on a shelf high up and to the left. She glanced upwards and away. During her brief moment of distraction I served her an adequate but not too harsh blow to the head with the truncheon-like legume I had been pretending to study. She keeled forward and collapsed onto the citrus fruit section.

"Mind the oranges..." I exclaimed, to no avail. Her body sprawled amid a cascade of all-natural Vitamin C providers. When the vendor rushed out, I slipped her ample recompense for the damaged goods. Then I popped Freida into a taxi, closing her hand around the vegetable of her demise, and sent her to the casualty ward of St. Margaret's New Hospital. Not that she needed any medical attention - Freida was tougher than most people and probably immortal. I merely thought it would be an amusing touch for her to wake up in hospital just like the last time we met.

Back at my home I quickly checked my video-mail. There weren't many messages, just a few advertising circulars which had penetrated my anti-junk filters, and a final ransom message for a stolen sports car which I'd long since received the insurance money for. I was reminded that I hadn't yet driven the McLaren F45 I'd had delivered a few days previously. The McLaren had been an impulse purchase while waiting at the bar for a free table in McDonalds. The new job made taxis more appropriate, so I hadn't found the opportunity to take my new vehicle for a spin. After unpacking my bags from my lunar trip, I went down to the garage and climbed into the sleek, sexual McLaren. The way things were going, there didn't seem much point in pretending I was a poor neuropsychologist anymore. I might as well live a little. Switching the Autoroute off, I drove manually to the COSI offices.

Carmichael was not available to see me, so I took the tapes from the Nexus-7 clinic and wired myself into a few of them. I was most interested in those subjects who had developed withdrawal of consciousness in adulthood rather than those who were born withdrawn. If you searched long enough, you could find some remnants of their former personalities, such as little memories of themselves at various ages, fragmented and hidden inside their minds. With von Kühnert there was nothing. It was like he had been drained of all non-physical aspects of himself. He was emptier than prime time entertainment.

I made an appointment to see Carmichael the following day, created backups of the discs from my research, and returned to the car park. I wondered if any of these low-paid COSI droids were curious how I could afford such an expensive land vehicle as the F45, with a purchase waiting list longer than a very long thing indeed. Most of them drove little Chinese electric cars that made a shopping trolley look like a Ferrari. After activating the gravitational security belt in the McLaren, I reached forward to turn off the Autoroute, which must have flicked on by accident the last time I got out. Without my bidding, the engine fired up and the car screeched off out of its space. The object sensors were keeping it from colliding with any walls or other vehicles, but otherwise it was negotiating its exit route from the COSI parking facilities more alarmingly than had even I been driving. I tried to lift my arm to disengage the Autoroute again. I had to use all the physical strength I could muster just to raise my hand. The flat-out acceleration combined with the uncomfortably high setting of the gravitational security kept me pressed to the seat.

The F-45 was burning past every other vehicle it met with ease, going completely not in the direction of my home. We headed south, over Westminster Bridge, jumping every traffic signal and forcing a number of other land cars off the road, including eight police vehicles and an ambulance. We seemed to be heading towards Peckham. As the car lunged left and right, I began to feel ill. Not so much as a result of the reckless driving, but because Southwark's shabby town planning made my stomach churn. Fumbling for my Pocket Assistant had proved pointless as the auto car shutdown I'd programmed merely succeeded in triggering a rendition of "The East is Red" fully orchestrated for retro wave-table MIDI. Somebody knew my little tricks and had programmed around them. I was stuck with this journey for the duration, and after a few miles the buffeting G-forces knocked me out. I loved fast cars, but I preferred driving them myself. I'd never been the best of passengers.

* * *

Sharp light was searing into my retina like a surgical water-jet. It was even painful when I shut my eyes, penetrating the lids as if they were rice-paper. Suddenly the light went out. I shook my head, as if simple head motion would return my vision more quickly. There was no way of telling just how long I'd been out. As the after burn from my initial blinding receded, a figure became clear standing in front of me. At first I had to blink, thinking my sight had been permanently damaged. The man had no nose. Otherwise normal, his face was very flat without its proboscis, which seemed to have been replaced by two holes on his cheeks that flared and vibrated like gills as he breathed. He grinned widely. Nothing abnormal about his mouth, luckily, or I might have retched.

"Mr Dean," the Man Who Had Cut Off His Nose to Spite His Face exclaimed enthusiastically. "We've been watching your activities for many years now. You're a rare breed, like us. A lawbreaker devious enough to avoid a criminal record! There are only a few of us around who manage to keep ourselves away from the grasp of the corporate database. When you die, which may be quite soon, we'll have you stuffed and displayed in a case, like one of our favourite pets."

"Fuck off," I grumbled, in no mood for banter. I was physically strapped to the chair, as well as gravitationally restrained. I cursed mankind's mastery of the six forces between atoms.

"For today's entertainment, we've brought round an old friend of yours," continued No Nose, stepping aside as a more familiar and visually pleasant work of surgical reconstruction entered through a door made of one-way glass. "I think you know Freida Eglin."

Freida seemed to be holding something phallic in her hand. As she approached it became clear: a courgette.

"I'm not going to make this easy for you, Bentley," she sniggered, brandishing the vegetable. Grasping my chair, which was designed to be rotated in all directions, she whirled it around until I was facing the floor. My nakedness, not normally something I minded when it occurred, now felt shatteringly frail. "If I didn't want to bear your children one day, I'd be slicing off your dick right now. Remember that as you gain intimate carnal knowledge of this vegetable." From that moment I knew I would never be able to enjoy another mouthful of ratatouille again.

"What a shame I forgot to bring any lubricating jelly," she chuckled as I winced. "I think it likes you," she added, ramming the courgette home

Upright again, I lost my temper. "Who the fuck is this other cunt?" I growled.

"He's from the League," Freida replied, making me none the wiser. "Unfortunately, these vegetable antics have nothing to do with what the League are about to do to you. But it was good for me!" With that Freida left the way she had come.

"So what's the League and how do I join?" I enquired, vainly doing my best to regain some composure and turn toward No Nose. "Is it some kind of sports club?"

"We are the League of Future Life, Mr Dean," replied No Nose without a hint of humour. That set off a blink of recognition. In the early days of genetic engineering and transplant surgery, religious anti-mutationists had killed a number of leading doctors in the two fields. The specialists had been accused of committing crimes against humankind. The weak-willed Central European government had bowed to extremist pressure and legislated against all transplant surgery, genetic engineering or prostheses that did not relate to returning a person to their fictional idea of "normal human health". But when strong human desires are made illegal, they go underground. Alongside strong human desires go large quantities of money. So a loose network was built up of doctors performing illegal research on medical processes for human augmentation and their rich, curious clientele. The hard core called themselves the League of Future Life. I'd only had dealings with those members of the League who'd had bits of computer equipment grafted into their skulls. The flesh link had made them natural, instinctive hackers and useful allies in electronic bank robbery. Freida must have become acquainted with the League via a different route – through her plastic surgeons.

"Do you wear a mask in polite company?" I asked. "I've often wondered how you guys keep it all a secret."

"You're a funny guy, Mr Dean, for someone with a courgette up his arse," said No Nose. I noticed traces of a German accent. "But we haven't really brought you here for an evening of comic entertainment. We are as aware as you of the import of these Mind Invasions. Somebody is doing their own research on the Pure Light Abacus, and then kicking the ladder away they've just climbed up to keep what they've learned exclusive. We will offer you substantially more than you ever made hacking American corporate bank accounts if you can help us obtain this Pure Light Abacus."

"I'll think about a deal with you if you take the courgette out of me before it makes me permanently flatulent," I offered. This was not quite the kind of business transaction I was used to. Vegetables were much healthier dry fried on ridged cast iron and made poor enemas, in my opinion.

Gingerly easing the vegetable out of me with his fingertips, No Nose hissed into my face, his breathing holes quivering:

"Cross us on this deal, and it will be a marrow full of explosives next time."

* * *

I was getting sick of meeting new people to work with, especially under such compromising circumstances. Behind the Mind Invasions were one or more attempts to obtain this powerful and mysterious supercomputer called the Pure Light Abacus. But none of my new business partners claimed to be doing the invasions themselves, so I was none the wiser. Back in my apartment, I finished off some new security viruses to prevent me being hijacked by my own car ever again. Then I hooked up to the Mind Strobe and explored a few famous psychoanalytic VR brain scans, according to my Dummy's Guide to the Cerebral Cortex. The prevailing theory was that the unconscious constructed a whole internal world like the real one. Imaginary buildings represented the innate constraints of symbolic communication. Cultural memories were stored in these buildings, not according to any overall theme, but grouped by association with each-other. Objects could reside in more than one building, folding each room into others in a complex multidimensional fashion. According to this theory, von Kühnert's featureless mental space was now devoid of all cultural learning. The most basic bit of culture was the sense of being separated from the world and conscious of oneself. He didn't even have that. Even the most addled living human had something in his or her building that belied some self-consciousness. Von Kühnert had been stripped bare.

I got into the COSI archive system and looked inside a few other Mind Invasion victims. They were all empty. Had they been wiped or had their conscious self somehow been extracted? I knew of no successful technology able to do this, but it seemed the only conclusion. The time had come to return to the office. By then the sun was setting and the city was beginning to become light as the holo-neons started to beam into the sky. Advertisements for custard replication chips to add to your cooker vied for attention with a global mood display which had been erected as public art. It projected fractals linked to the world emotion index onto a huge phosphorescent arch. Everybody must have been angry at that moment because the patterns were predominately red. Perhaps they didn't like custard.

Back at the office I got a pass and some VR brain equipment and went to see von Kühnert. He looked a little different from the last time we'd met. For a start, he was emitting gentle cooing noises and playing with some highly coloured objects which a nurse had brought him. Personally, I'd preferred him before. He started to cry when I attached the VR probe, so I had him tranquillised. Once inside, I found his mind's building was no longer empty. It struck me as strange that none of the other reports on Mind Invasion victims mentioned any convalescence. The passageways inside von Kühnert were now similar colours to his plastic shapes, and the rooms were taking on circular and round architectural motifs. There was a constant babble everywhere I explored, just above the audible level. No words seemed discernible, however.

I didn't stay long. It was obvious von Kühnert was re-experiencing childhood. Pretty soon this would obliterate any traces of his former personality. So that meant it was pointless trying to reconstruct anything to find who'd stolen his mind. By the time we'd gotten anything out of him of his old self he might even be walking and saying "dada" – most probably to me. This was a thought worth very little consideration. Children ranked alongside poor people as my least favourite companions. It all came from my being bullied at school for not being able to afford new trousers. At least, that was my story and I was sticking to it.

In my office I took another look at archival material of Mind Invasion cases. There were no records of research after about two or three days of the victims' returning from kidnapping. It was all falling into place. From what I dimly remembered of neuropsychology from a few documentaries, it was presently possible to reconstruct memories from a recently deceased brain. You couldn't yet reanimate people once they were dead, but you could find out what they had experienced during most of their lives. Rich people had their deceased loved ones' minds recorded onto 3D videocassettes. Many murderers were now convicted by the reconstructed memories of their victims. Even if you diced and cooked a person's brain in a red wine-flavoured sauce it was still possible to get something from the marinated bits.

However, in the case of von K and the other Mind Invasions, by letting them live once their memories had been taken, the thieves allowed the natural living and learning processes to erase all traces of their former experiences. The new data overwrote the old. By the Law of the Mutual Exclusivity of the Entropy of Self, the new beings could be totally different from the old, as genetics only dictated so much, the rest coming from the experience of choosing your way in the world. This was an elegant and inspired method of covering your tracks, if you asked me. Why it took a non-scientist such as myself to realise it was a mystery. Well, actually it wasn't. Only a devious criminal could guess the motives of a devious criminal. I recorded a video message for Vanessa Carmichael about my findings, strongly encrypted it, and headed for home. The next day I intended to visit some of the other Mind Invasions in person to confirm my suspicions.

With a shudder, I realised I was starting to enjoy this COSI job. Gainful employment had never been one of my life goals, and the fun I was having made me feel a little dirty.

Log 000011011010 – Language is a virus from outer space – you'd rather hear your name than see your face. Humans can't cope with direct experience, and would rather have a representation of reality than the thing itself. Since mankind likes to worship the symbols generated by its own imagination, people can be led to believe anything that fits their interpretation. This is a very useful thing if you know how to take advantage of it.

My concern about the security of my Islington home received a further blow when I awoke, feeling refreshed by a deep sleep. The intruder alarms were all off and sitting at the end of my bed I found the last person I wanted to spend time with, even after children and poor people. Most red-blooded males would have had trouble refusing the plastic glory of Freida Eglin, but I had no intention of waking up with my own genitalia where a courgette had recently been. Today she was a bouncy redhead. For once she was wearing underwear - obviously just for the effect when she took it off. She looked as well rendered as a Disney cartoon. I pulled my handgun from under the pillow.

"That wasn't the weapon I was hoping to see," Freida remarked, coyly, unlacing the front of her scanty black top. Her hand reached inside and she began to touch herself enticingly. It wouldn't have been sensible to kill her in my own house, so I went over to the cupboard and retrieved a magazine of tranqs from inside. I turned back towards Freida only to be greeted with a different set of barrels from the ones I had expected. The gun was curiously huge, and where she'd been hiding it was almost as big a mystery. Before I could even open my mouth she'd shot me. There was no hole in my chest or prick from a narcotic soluble needle - just a scarcely audible click and then my body crumpled around me. The gun was a sonic device that worked on the human nervous system, setting up an interference wave which jammed the information flow along the nerves. I remained conscious, able only to blink and breathe as Freida lifted me off the ground, undressed me, and tied me to the bedposts. I should never have bought an antique brass four-poster.

Freida left the bedroom. Chopping and other sundry culinary sounds made their way through the open door, most likely coming from the kitchen. Then Freida returned with a shiny round object like a miniature black Edam cheese and placed it over my solar plexus. A touch of the centre and she'd counteracted the sonic gun and given me back my nervous system. She put the electric cheese aside and grasped my manhood, removing the remainder of her clothing with her free hand. I just lay there. I was pretty sure she preferred it like that anyway.

"Ooh, that's great," I said ironically as she began to give out short gasps. In fact, she wasn't bad. After all, she'd had decades of practice - probably from a very early age, too. She was rumoured to have earned her first few paycheques that way.

Afterwards, she untied me and led me at gunpoint to the dining room. Binding me once more, this time to a chair, she muttered something about "what a girl has to go through to get an evening of romance", and fetched a dish from the kitchen. The table was already laid. Placing the dish in front of me she untied my hands and told me to serve. Then she lit some candles, dimmed the lights, and sat opposite me across the table, gun in hand.

"You look gorgeous," she cooed. I nodded, feeling that something wasn't quite right with this evening of love. Maybe the ambient light was a little bright, maybe the lack of music was ruining the mood, or maybe it was because we were both still naked, my legs were tied to a chair, and there was a weird gun pointed straight at me. Inside the dish, of course, was vegetarian food. Not surprisingly, courgette parmigiana.

"Oh, Jesus, this isn't the same one, is it?" I complained, feeling the whole situation had become a little tiresome.

"No!!!" exclaimed Freida. "I've already eaten that one..."

Feeling thoroughly reassured, I served the food and we had dinner.

* * *

Before I explain how I got out of that situation, let me first underline that I had already begun to wonder about how fast my investigation was going. How had I learnt so much about mind invasions when other investigators had failed (and in some cases, died)? Brilliant as I was at robbing banks, I doubted my neurological skill were so accomplished. Yet the situation so far seemed rather obvious and logical. I felt like a powerful secret organisation could see my obvious uses and was helping me along.

I was wrong.

When the robot assassins broke into my flat, I was still tied to the chair. Freida went straight for her gun but her fingers didn't even reach the hand grip before she was flung backwards by an explosive shell which blasted her expensively-augmented chest into tiny pieces. It was a good thing she was already dead when she hit the floor as the sorrow of seeing her plastic surgeon's masterpiece ruined would have killed her anyway. That split second while the robots had their attention on her was enough for me to shout the word which activated my anti-automaton nano-security. The flea-sized swarm engulfed both the robots and in a matter of seconds one of them had toppled. The other, realising that I was the originator of this almost invisible attack let off a shot, but had already lost most of its sensory apparatus so succeeded only in blowing a huge hole in the ceiling above my head. In less than a minute, the nano-security had broken down the robots to their constituent materials and rebuilt them into a pair of simulated Adirondack chairs, as it had been programmed to. You could always use extra period furniture, after all.

Further explosions coming from the corridor outside my apartment made me realise that the two robots were just the advance party. After a concerted effort, I managed to get out of Freida's badly-tied bonds and quickly grabbed some clothes, my pocket assistant and a gun. Then I jumped down the garbage chute. Fortunately, this was a new model chute with a gravitational brake to prevent refuse falling too fast and causing a mess at the bottom. In the basement, I wiped the decaying refuse off my still-naked body and put on the clothes. I punched a few code numbers into my pocket assistant. These deactivated all the rear security of the building, enabling me to escape into the garden. I was greeted by some very badly-aimed blue beams, which succeeded only in biting out a few chunks of the wall above me. There were two men and a woman, all dressed in black and wearing fully-enclosed riot helmets. Each carried a light assault laser. They can't have been well trained, or probably weren't expecting me, as I was able to take out all three at once by shooting the man in the middle with a poison flechette grenade, an ammunition outlawed a decade previously but still readily available if you knew where to look. It was a nasty weapon but highly effective. The detonation tore the central policeman in half and filled the two either side with needles of toxin which incapacitated them in seconds. I leapt over the wall and into the next garden, and then through some more gardens until I was in a back alley. They obviously hadn't been expecting me to survive the robots, because nobody was waiting for me there at all. Too much faith was put in technology, and not enough in people. The jump-jet that had been over my house the whole time was still hovering, flailing a searchlight about as the pilot tried to work out what had gone wrong. I hurried away from the scene and set off for King's Cross, although I didn't think much of my chances of blending in amongst prostitutes and the homeless clothed in the relatively new DKNY leisurewear I'd managed to grab from my flat.

Mind you, I did reek of mouldy vegetables and rancid meat bones, and I was definitely now homeless, so perhaps King's Cross was an appropriate place for me. After ten minutes or so of walking, I turned off the Euston Road onto a back street. The occasional corner-loitering female eyed me with intent to do business. They didn't look half bad. Cosmetic surgery had become so cheap as to be given away with breakfast cereal, so the overall visual standard of prostitutes had gone up. Bargain-basement knife work had its long-term drawbacks, though, and life expectancy had fallen somewhat as a result. The moral majority, a misnomer as they had become a political minority, seemed to think it served the girls right for committing a carnal sin.

I hit upon an idea. Scouting around the area, I found an innocent and young-looking whore, probably barely over 18, and casually approached her. She seemed very pleased to see me until I was within smelling distance, and then the reek of the rubbish tip kicked in. To reassure her, I pulled out my Smartcash chit and waved it like a white flag. I'd only just checked my credit rating with my pocket assistant, so I knew I still had plenty of money. Nobody had sent any viruses to scramble my funds as yet. I explained the situation:

"I'd like you all night - the full works," I began. The girl pulled out her Cash Reader and stated her terms.

"700,000 now and 700,000 afterwards plus a customer-defined tip."

Since prostitution had been legalised, ladies of the night had been able to take advantage of vastly improved credit and financial management systems. However, because some customers preferred the sleaze, there was still a market for "shop fronts" in squalid areas like King's Cross. The dark lights and liberally-strewn debris could really improve a girl's appearance in a way much more seductive than sculpted, injected breasts and lips. Fantasy would always beat reality, any day, especially when it came to sexual gratification. I soon learned that my new friend for the night called herself Michelle and was of Northern origin. Up in her room I suggested that if I could tie her up I'd give her extra. She must have been hard up because she only wanted 100,000 more ECUs on her cash reader before I was strapping her to the bedposts with her suspenders. Then I pulled out the gas syringe I'd found earlier in my DKNY jacket and tranquillised her. It was handy to leave such things in your spare clothing just in case.

I figured the Sleep Juice Special injection would last about eight hours, so I got cracking on my PDA and started to look for information on the Pure Light Abacus. What I'd learnt from Harry of the Thai Free State was that this was a new kind of computer, the design of which was distilled from the cream of research into lasers, fibre optics and neural nets. The machine's main processor was made up of vessels of inert gases under very high pressure, though not high enough to render them liquid. The chaotic motion of the gases could be partially controlled by blue lasers, and the gas chaos followed certain non-linear laws. Under higher pressure and manipulated using electro-magnetic forces, the behaviour of the gases could be expressed as calculable formulas. Hence, a massively parallel computational device could be formed. The gases emitted different-coloured light according to their structure, and changed this structure according to the frequency and pattern of light that was being fed in. Thus a feedback loop which worked as a neural net was set up and the computer could learn, relaying answers to the questions posed at the other end of the tube in light form. Because the gas computer worked at the atomic and molecular level, its processing power by volume was beyond anything ever created before.

Of course, all this was conjecture as nobody had been able to get the thing to work at low enough pressures to be manageable. Quite a few researchers had died in an explosion in Russia. The phosphorescing gases that had escaped emitted large quantities of ultraviolet light and burnt the researchers to a crisp. The company responsible never returned to computer technology and instead developed a market-leading brand of sun beds. Other organisations around the world had managed to get prototypes to work, but only with synthetic gases too ridiculously expensive to manufacture for a viable commercial product. The biggest problem was maintaining pressure without causing the gases to liquefy, which killed the computation.

The info agent in my personal assistant also retrieved details of a novel Gaia-offshoot theory that the phenomenal pressures in a planet's core created a "gas brain" of the Pure Light Abacus type. According to the theory, gases which were trapped under the solid sections of a planet's mantle could develop independent thought, giving Mother Earth a mind of her own. By this logic, black holes and white dwarves were super genii not supernovae. Another interesting titbit I discovered concerned how the Church of Scientology had used the money it had won from Microsoft for copyright infringement, after winning many other cases against the free dissemination of its doctrine. It had invested heavily in research into high pressure gas optic computers (aka HPGOCs), like the Abacus. Microsoft had lost the case against the Church over its Ron operating system, which forced users subliminally to operate no other software than Microsoft's and cost more time and money the more you understood it. A clear case of plagiarism.

The R&D centre doing the most successful research at that time into HPGOCs was the Mao Tse Tung AI Unit in the Duty Free State of Andorra, between France and Spain. These small countries were very popular with shady research establishments because they had to attract industry somehow other than with the promise of an inexpensive workforce. Instead, they relaxed their laws. Andorra had even left the European Union. In federalist Europe, small states were dictated to by the EC parliament. So much for the miracle of proportional representation. The MTT company had been set up by Mao's entrepreneurial great granddaughter in order to blend communist theory with empowered management in the high tech industry. Her mega corporation had many R&D centres in the countries where nobody legislated against contamination.

This selection of informational morsels didn't seem to be enough for all the intrigue and killing - although people had been known to murder each other over a Phil Collins original. In fact, there was a famous case of this popularly known as the Full Metal Jacket Required Murders, which was an amusing journalistic play on the album title and type of ammo used in the killing. I centred my research onto Andorra and widened the parameters to include recent news reports. Apparently, there had been a failed takeover bid of MTT AI by a Singaporean firm in the last two weeks. In fact, considering how non-lucrative HPGOCs looked as a commercial venture, what with the instability of the technology, there had been a lot of takeover bids during the last year. Pepsico had made a failed attempt as had BMW. In all cases, the business reasons for failure were almost as mysterious as why anyone was interested in the technology in the first place. Although the importance of super computing power to Pepsi's "Uh-huh" space programme was obvious, the viability of vehicles running on gas fuel with a mind of its own was questionable. I flicked the switch on the PDA to the off position.

Michelle looked cherubic as she lay drugged, strapped hand and foot. I was tempted to get my money's worth, although I hated people who forced themselves on women without their consent. Instead, I stripped off my socks and took them with the rest of my clothes into the bathroom, which conveniently housed a Dirtblaster laser washer drier. After I'd rinsed the last whiff of fetid cabbage from my body in the RazorJet shower cubicle, I reached for the bar of soap Michelle must have purchased three weeks previously when retro bathing had most recently been fashionable. The water force shield suddenly dropped and I was staring down the barrel of my own gun. I must admit I let out an inadvertent whimper. This was more from amusement than anything, as it was only Michelle holding the gun. Her finger wasn't even on the trigger properly. Less than four hours had passed since I'd injected her. She must have been grown in a vat. The strong constitution engineered in bodies grown outside the womb interfered with the workings of the Sleep Juice Special, amongst other things.

"Hey, you're up", was all I could manage to say without laughing.

"Yes, you fuck," replied my pubescent northern Lolita. "What the fuck did you do to me? I said you could tie me up, not tranq me. Tranqing is fucking extra." She'd miraculously been transformed into a true vulgarian.

I'd made my mind up. Andorra had to be investigated. Whether I was still a COSI employee or not, which seemed questionable after the recent chain of events, my remaining alive hinged on finding out what was going on with the Mind Invasions and how this was linked to the Pure Light Abacus. If I found out something valuable it might help keep me alive. Messing about with a female resident of Kings Cross was diverting but the fun was over. I put on my sweetest smile.

"I'm sorry, Michelle, I didn't realise. If you'll just let me dry off, I'll reimburse you."

She didn't like that idea. She asked me what I was doing with the "mini screen", presumably referring to my PDA. It was a little overconfident of me to leave it on her bedroom table. I told her I liked to look at movies to turn me on. She didn't believe me.

"You've got too much money. You're a vice agent. Tell me what's up or I'll bleep the cops. I've got customers in the force and they'll look after me. I get a cop call-out quicker than a pizza delivery. So what's going on?!"

This was starting to be annoying. Now I had to silence her because somebody much more professional than Michelle was out to kill me and pretty soon they'd find this girl and know where I'd been. With a little pursing of the lips I began:

"I'm an agent. You're right. I'm investigating the use of copyrighted custom breast shapes from virtual sex salons. This is a convenient place for me to work undercover. I was expecting you to be unconscious for some time so I could get out on the street and use the scanner installed in my retina to check some breasts. There are quite a few women around here who have designer boobs in styles copied from the custom curves of my fashion-world clients. They're infringing copyright and they must be brought to justice!"

Michelle nodded sagely. "That's total crap and you know it," she commented, still nodding her head.

"Look," I began, trying to appear concerned. "Let me show you what I'm talking about. I'll call up the latest Versace nipple and you can tell me if you know anybody who's got one." Then I added: "Can I at least dry off?"

She motioned acceptance and I touched the dry toggle on the RazorJet. The water droplets evaporated from my skin like time lapse photography. Still under the watchful muzzle of my own gun, I retrieved my clothing from the Dirtblaster and pulled on my Microsoft chip-controlled silk boxers. This was very user-friendly underwear, but the fly occasionally popped open unexpectedly and for no apparent reason. With the rest of my clothing over my arm, we trouped back to the bedroom. I tried small talk.

"So you were grown in a vat? I never quite understood how that worked with the whole Freudian kill your father thing. Did you have adolescent feelings of rebellion towards racks of test tubes?"

Michelle looked rather aggravated. "I never had an adolescence."

Perhaps it would have actually been good for this girl if I'd killed her. She seemed unhappy. As I pored over the PDA, I kept vigilant for her to drop her guard. She was good for an amateur. Very attentive. But I was a pro.

I called up a graphic I'd found months back of interactive male star Rod Fletcher standing in Hugh Grant Square, right outside in Kings Cross. That grabbed Michelle's attention for a split second. Rod had never been to the Square, of course. It was a retouched holoimage. Rod would never have done a bad thing like cruise around for a prostitute. Before she knew what had happened I had my gun back in my hand. Michelle was rubbing her forearm where I'd whacked a pressure point to make her release her grip on the weapon before she pulled the trigger. I pointed the gun at her.

Michelle looked crestfallen. I smiled. I wasn't exactly sure what I was going to do. I badly wanted to go to Andorra but something about this girl made me not want to kill her immediately. I had few qualms about killing people if they'd earned it - sometimes even if they just got in the way and it was necessary. Michelle, however, didn't deserve to die. She seemed a cut above the average teenage prostitute. I had a hunch she might come in handy for something, although I wasn't sure what. But how did you keep a woman quiet who was resistant to Sleep Juice Special? There were a couple of shots left in the syringe. Despite reduced effectiveness, this would have to do for now. I told her to take off her underwear and lie face down on the bed.

"I don't do Greek!" she hissed. I just ignored her and stamped her on the buttock with the syringe.

When I'd dressed us both, I considered my options for Andorra. I had four choices - air transport, sea, channel tunnel, or I could take the bridge to continental Europe. I opted for buying a personal skycar with some of my spare cash, no questions asked. A brief foray into the Friendlybank virtual shopping mall got me a great deal on a new sports two-seater with Stealth ECM. Under an anonymous encrypted name, I took delivery of the vertical take off automobile in Hugh Grant Square two hours later. I loaded the sleeping Michelle into the passenger seat and strapped her down firmly so she couldn't cause any more trouble when she awoke in a couple of hours.

The skycar locked into 3D traffic control. ECM Stealth registered us as Mrs Maud Bristol off to visit relatives. Fortunately, crooked politicians with dodgy deals to hide had managed to prevent adequate ID on a world-wide scale. If you knew the system you could pretend to be almost anybody. Various brands of digital cash were as anonymous as physical cash used to be, and since that's all I used nobody could trace me. Or so the theory went.

Log 000001010111 – Now that so much of human activity is dictated by databases, you can change the course of history simply by altering a few entries in a file or two. The whole of human life rests upon trusting information from accredited sources, and a small amount of falsified data can trigger any action you want.

After four hours of flying we touched down in the Mao Tse Tung AI Unit car park. I'd had to use up the last shot in the Sleep Juice syringe on Michelle. I left her in the skycar, sleeping like a baby - well, a baby wearing too much makeup and an indecently short skirt. Strangely, there was no guard at the main entrance. I flipped open my PDA and retrieved the auto-unlock code for the doors from an on-line hacker store. The code only cost a few ECUs. The black market had benefited particularly well from electronic shopping, making any hacking information you needed just a credit card away. The door opened and I entered the building. All was unnaturally silent. Perhaps everyone took their lunch breaks at the same time. I was surprised they hadn't brought sandwiches and worked through the break, or at least ordered pizza. This was supposed to be a scientific establishment, after all, and there was virtually nowhere good to eat in Andorra anymore. European free trade had taken away the country's only real selling point - duty free goods. That part of Andorra's history had become just a memory when the last corner shop selling sheepskin and leather closed for business over a generation previously. The only way the Andorran government could tempt any industry other than skiing was by loosening the environmental laws compared to France or Spain.

At the first hallway inside the Mao Tse Tung AI Unit I discovered a double set of doors swinging open, half off their hinges. The spotlessly clean corridor beyond led to a changing room lined with lockers containing special clothing. This was obviously required wearing for entrance into the laboratory. Not wanting to look out of place inside, I changed into one of these orange boiler suits. I was still carrying my gun, however, and if I had to use it I'd probably cause a little more damage than the dust on my shoes. Within the airlock little automatic vacuum cleaners sucked off stray particles and a few red lights flashed, accompanied by a tinny automatic voice which warned me that I was carrying potentially dangerous explosives. Past the airlock into the Clean Area, I found another empty reception. The screens behind the desk were dead, but I was able to hook up my PDA to a network node and get into the system. I called up a building schematic. There were various rooms devoted to intelligent agent research, something called the "Soul Randomizer", and some robotics labs. There was also a large room with just a serial number instead of a contents description. The MTT AI scientists were obviously none too subtle when they wanted something kept secret. This could only have been the home of the Pure Light Abacus.

Up on the next floor I found the unmarked room. It wasn't hard - there were three very crispy-looking charred Chinese corpses trailed like a paper chase along the corridor straight to the room from the stairwell. At least, I assumed they were Chinese from their general size and build. I drew my gun, but there was nobody alive inside, just more crispy Orientals. The large lab was octagonal in shape, with a high ceiling and a couple of steps leading down on all sides to a central hole. A few wires trailed out of the gap giving the impression something had been ripped out in a fairly indiscriminate fashion. A console on one side of the room faced inwards. While I was trying to figure out what had been tested in the centre of the space I heard a girl shrieking in the corridor. There were other voices. I flattened myself against the wall next to the door. The voices became discernible. First, a girl who sounded rather like Michelle:

"Get your bloody hands off me. I don't have any idea what I'm doing here, wherever here is. I was kidnapped by some pervert who keeps injecting me with some tranq drug. I don't know where he's gone now. I was asleep, see?" Another voice cut in coolly at this point, and I felt a glimmer of recognition.

"No need to grab her arm so tightly, Darryl. She's no match for you."

The group entered the lab through the open door. Before anybody could react I stepped forward and exclaimed, "Nobody moves." It was the kind of corny statement I liked to make in these kinds of circumstances. Then I recognised a few faces. The cool voice was Harry of the Thai Free State. Santada was with him as before, this time sporting some kind of wearable computer jump-suit. The one known as Darryl I didn't recognise. Sure enough, he had Michelle by the arm, and she was half-heartedly trying to wriggle free.

"Ah, Mr Dean. I had a gut feeling I would find you sneaking behind a door somewhere. We met your girlfriend outside."

Michelle took this as a cue. "This is the pervert I was talking about. What is all this crap?" But everyone was ignoring her, which only served to increase her indignation.

"Harry," I began. "I assume this was where the Pure Light Abacus you were telling me about used to live?"

"Yes, but it looks like somebody else got here first, hmm?" answered Harry, stating the obvious as if it was a closely guarded secret. He didn't appear too unhappy that the Abacus was nowhere to be found, but then he was the kind of guy who would wear a smile in pretty much every situation.

"You do realise how many different organisations and groups are after this thing? Apart from COSI, there's the League of Future Life. There must be some Americans, too, and the New Soviets probably have an interest as well. If you ask me, everybody's jumping on everybody else's train." I'd let my creative imagination run away with me there, but it didn't sound too farfetched considering the smoking wreckage around us. This was definitely something more important than just the theft of a few scientific minds and a big computer.

One group I hadn't mentioned in my imaginative list of interested parties was the Chinese. Considering that the Abacus had clearly just been stolen from one of their facilities, and a number of their nationals killed in the process, the Chinese were likely to be not just interested but downright concerned. Although communism in China had long since evolved into something Karl Marx would have had trouble recognising, Chinese corporations were still something very different from Western ones. Not only did companies like MMT make everything under the sun, they behaved more like military organisations or religious cults. They were a law unto themselves. It was already surprising that a Chinese company had been raided like this, but it would be even more of a surprise if they didn't do something about it very quickly. We would have to move fast to track down the Abacus before MMT's own operatives retrieved it.

I could smell an acrid aroma beginning to filter into the room. It wasn't coming from the singed bodies, but instead reeked of ozone as if some wires had shorted out badly. The stench was getting worse. The neon lighting flickered momentarily. Acting on a hunch I hooked my PDA wirelessly into the only still-working console in the lab and hacked into the building-wide diagnostic. A number of power circuits at the facility had malfunctioned and were now overloading, causing multiple electrical fires. I tried to track the reason for the overload. It appeared to have been programmed into the power control computer a few weeks previously, I discovered, and was being triggered remotely. It was as if someone knew we were coming and had prepared a little welcome. I traced the transmissions to a small local area network in America. It seemed to be situated somewhere in New York City, but there wasn't time for further research. The overload was spreading, and it wouldn't be long before an uncontrollable inferno erupted right where we were standing.

"Let's go, Harry." I began. "This place will be a furnace very soon and I don't have much faith in the Andorran fire department."

The corridor was full of evil-smelling smoke. We made our way back to the entrance, which had mysteriously fused shut. Harry's man Darryl revealed some Nanotech plastic which he quickly shaped around the door before setting off the reaction. Within seconds the tiny molecular robots ate a path through the door and then regrouped into a ball on the other side. We kicked our way through with ease, then Darryl retrieved his Nanotech and we moved outside into the car park.

I turned to the group.

"Harry, it's been great seeing you, but this is where Michelle and I will have to love you and leave you. Keep in touch, okay? It really has been terrific seeing you again."

"Mr Dean-ah," Harry intoned in that sing-song South East Asian way. "Remember we had an agreement."

"And we still do, Harry old son, it's just that I need to work out what's going on here. Somebody blew up my house! I had some priceless art works and my complete collection of antique Jerry Springer videos in there. I'm really pissed off, Harry, and I don't mind telling you somebody's going to have their buttocks grated off with a hand blender when I find out who's responsible." I grabbed Michelle by the wrist and began to make my way towards the skycar. Then I had second thoughts and let her go. She'd have gotten in the way, even if a bit of casual sex here and there might have passed the time in transit.

"Sweety, you'd be better off with Harry and his gang. They might even take you home." Michelle scurried off.

A few minutes later, as I was going through a system check on the vehicle, she reappeared.

"Hey, Mr Dean. You couldn't drop me home, could you?"

"I'm afraid I'm not the school bus, dear. I'm sure you could strike up trade here and make enough money to get back in a very short time. Little girls like you are in hot demand. Or what about Harry?"

"He gave me this," she chirped, raising a small pistol in my general direction.

I nodded sagely, as if agreeing with a well-reasoned argument. Feeling resigned to having a travelling partner, I inquired "Have you ever been to America?"

Log 000001110101 – What's the magic word? The magic word is the one that makes people do something. Say the magic word and people will perform your bidding. It's one of the mysteries of life how language and action are connected. What do we have to say to make people kill each other?

Eight hours of hard driving and we were in New York. Well, the autopilot did the hard driving - Michelle and I did the hard sleeping. The only part of the journey that required any real effort from me was handing the keys to the parking attendant at the Central Queens Park'n'Ride. I felt stiff from the small passenger compartment, but other than that it had been a model journey.

"Which one of you is Maaard Bristol?" inquired the feckless payment booth attendant in a thick Brooklyn drawl. Giving the lad my most impatient, tired glance, I answered, "It's not really going to be me, is it? I'm Mr Bristol, and this is my wife Maud."

"There's a message waiting for Mrs Bristol, sir, is all. You can get it from the office on the way out." This was curious. Maud Bristol was a person I'd invented around twelve hours previously, simply for use with the skycar. It should have taken a little longer than that to trace the fictional identity to me, unless this was a pure case of coincidence. I squeezed my chin in thought for a second, my elbow lightly brushing my jacket where the gun was. The slight bulge was absentmindedly reassuring. Then Michelle and I strolled to the Park'n'Ride main office. A fat, greasy blob of a man went into the back to retrieve the message. He reminded me somewhat of Chucky, whose cerebrum I'd spattered over the Moon clinic. Perhaps he was a distant relative. The note arrived, scribbled on an antiquated square of paper with gum along one edge. All it said was, "You are the one". I turned the note over to see if the sender's name was on the back. Frowning, I asked the grease ball whether he knew who the message was from. He shrugged and growled, "Some guy, he didn't say".

"I guess you're the one, Maud," I said to Michelle.

Troubled by the strange message, I led Michelle out of the Park'n'Ride onto 35th Avenue. Customs and immigration were performed automatically as you entered most countries, so there were no longer any passport queues to wait in nor goods to declare. Electronic tagging documented your whereabouts and what valuable items you were carrying as you crossed national boundaries. Duties for goods shipped across economic zones were levied automatically, and if you didn't have the correct visa for entering a country you'd be tracked and apprehended before even reaching your destination. It all seemed deceptively uninhibited for travel, whereas in reality the system was repressively intrusive of your privacy. You couldn't go anywhere or move any item between countries without somebody knowing about it. Unless, of course, you hacked the system as I had done, and were travelling under a false identity with Stealth ECM selective jamming equipment. This registered our identities as whoever I said we were, and hid any illegal possessions, such as the explosive rounds in my handgun. US customs thought I was carrying a regular automatic .45 – the US government's basic minimum-required sidearm for all visitors to America. It was no longer legal to travel in the US unarmed.

The yellow cab I hailed on 35th Avenue was driven by an Amazonian pygmy, still wearing his jungle loincloth and a grimy Kentucky Fried Chicken tee-shirt. He spoke what seemed to be a sum total of two English words – "very" and "nice" – with which he managed to concoct a seemingly limitless array of verbal combinations. Unfortunately, he couldn't read the Spanish street signs nor understand the addresses either. It was lucky that American yellow cabs were equipped with holographic maps that were accessible to the passenger as well as the driver. I knew where I was going, and directed the diminutive taxi driver's every turn with hand gestures, backed up by commendations of "nice" and "very nice" whenever he swerved the right way.

Eventually we made it to Washington Square Park. I was feeling hungry, and so was Michelle. We stopped at Famous Ray's pizza for a slice. This was the original Famous Ray's, or so the façade said - "accept no substitute". It certainly was the most originally greasy and disgusting pizza I'd had since I was last in New York, but at least it didn't have pineapple on it. We drank Cola Beyond, which was clear and tasted almost like water because it had had the caffeine, sugar, colouring, and most of the flavouring removed. They were all bad for your health, you see. Satisfied, or at least filled up with substances that could just about pass as digestible, we departed for New York University's Gore Library. I was planning to hack the university's network connection to see if I could trace the source of the commands I'd discovered in Andorra. University networks were always the easiest way to get a local high-bandwidth connection when you needed one fast. You had to be a student to get into the library, and it cost a few dollars a visit, but I'd got it covered already during our journey by obtaining a wealthy Arab's ID string from an anonymous pirate newsgroup. Close scrutiny would probably have ascertained that I was not a twenty-year-old Qatarian parapsychology student, but close scrutiny was unlikely with the volume of students entering and leaving the library at any one time – even in the middle of the night. That was always the best thing about New York – night and day were only distinguishable by the level of light. It was brighter at night time.

As we were crossing Washington Square Park towards the Gore Library, my sixth sense told me someone was following us. The fact that the park was full of crazy people whacked out on drugs made it hard to be sure, but somehow I felt that one of the hundreds of human bodies in my peripheral vision had been there since we left the Park'n'Ride. For decades people had congregated in Washington Square to chat, mostly young people and mostly under the influence of some chemical substance or other. A few kids were showing off their hover board skills. A couple of glances around the park and my attention settled on a figure in a hooded coat made of ribbed aluminium. This was not the best attire for remaining inconspicuous, and probably a little warm for the delightful Spring day that currently blessed the Big Apple. I decided to leave the matter until after my research.

Inside the NYU library we sat down at a spare terminal on the third floor. The original building had been gutted and reconfigured as a centralised physical access point for a completely virtual collection of originally paper-based tomes. The real books were now stored under precisely climate-controlled conditions in a vault somewhere outside the city. Although you could access much of the information from the comfort of your own terminal anywhere in the world - even using a wireless cranial implant - access to some material was still restricted to the library. More important, however, was the peace and quiet the library's environs afforded. Despite all the advancements in making virtualisation more real, some physical experiences still couldn't be faked. Sex was best performed in person, unless you were a telecommunications sex fetishist – teledildophilia, they called it - or you enjoyed the company of vacuum cleaners. A good night out drinking couldn't really be simulated by opening up a bottle of Bud Heavy and ensconcing yourself next to a home netcam terminal, although quite a lot of people did just that. And libraries, although no longer where the books were stored, were still the best places to find high powered, fast access to academic information in an environment where you wouldn't be disturbed.

This was why I'd chosen a library to do my New York hacking. Powering on the Moon Microsystems terminal, I ran the fake library card through the verification slot. The message "Welcome to NYU Gore Library, Mohamed Al-Jafar" flashed up on the display. Then the antiquated iconic GUI appeared. I pulled up a text command Window, accessed my anonymous net-based repository of hacker software, and ran a few little applications that would take the trace I'd made in Andorra and attempt to continue it retrospectively here in New York. The hacker applications were able to do this by taking advantage of a secret backdoor into the UN's Herbivore surveillance system. Herbivore had made life very easy for criminals like me.

Herbivore kept tabs on everything, so whether you wanted to spy on your kids' choice of TV viewing or the whereabouts of your next assassination victim, a Herbivore hack could deliver the goods. It was the perfect reference, kept permanently up to date by the finest in spook software. As I busied myself at my terminal retrieving what I needed from Herbivore, Michelle sat at the terminal next to me and stared out the nearby window.

"I guess this isn't as bad as screwing lots of sad old men. You do realise that you get a reduced rate for keeping me multiple days?" She mused.

"Perhaps we should work out a little deal." I countered. "You could make a lot of money if you set up in America – they love an English accent over here. You can swear like a trooper and they'll still think you're a member of the Royal Family. I know a few people. I could sort something out. Right now, though, I need to get on with this." I turned away and was surprised to find Michelle didn't disturb me. She switched on the terminal in front of her and started to browse the services requiring no authentication. The Versace tribute channel seemed to hold her attention most.

It took a good hour before I'd pinpointed a building in Soho, which had originally got its name because it was the part of New York City south of a street called Houston. Since then the name was more commonly used by the African-American community as a reference to the number of prostitutes to be found in the neighbourhood. "SO many HOs" was what it now stood for. Soho appeared to be where the command that triggered the Mao Tse Tung conflagration had emanated from. Perhaps someone with a few answers was still down there. I logged off the terminal and motioned to Michelle that we were going. While I'd been finishing off my research, she'd moved on from browsing the latest fashion tips to researching vat-grown children.

"So you know you're a clone?" I asked. It turned out that Michelle had escaped from a medical test facility about two years previously. She'd been cultivated in a Newcastle-based lab owned by the Monsignor medical company. Her foetus had been genetically modified for testing an unknown new surgical process. Use of clones as guinea pigs was strictly illegal, but so lucrative that the fines applied for infringements were not a deterrent to the big medical and pharmaceutical corporations. During her escape, Michelle had blinded a scientist who'd been treating her like a lab rat, taken some money, then run as far as she could. She'd ended up in King's Cross. The choice was easy between a slow death as various bits of her were infected with disease, then perhaps cured, or doing tricks for a living. Being fucked was far better than being fucked up. A legitimate life was out of the question – she'd have been easily traced. And reporting to the authorities would have been a quick suicide, as she'd almost certainly have ended back at the lab. No wonder she'd noticeably cheered up now we were out of England.

It was still sunny when we departed the Gore library. No sooner had we left the entrance hall, when I noticed the glint of the ribbed aluminium puffa jacket.

"Wait here," I ordered Michelle, then strode towards the coat wearer, who faltered a second and then turned to hurry off. I sprinted after and rugby-tackled my prey to the ground. The aluminium coat made a clatter as it hit the pavement. Kneeling on the struggling figure's stomach, I threw back the hood. Underneath was one of the larger surprises I've had in my life.

"Hello, my little zucchini," said Freida. "I thought zucchini would be a more appropriate nickname than 'courgette' as we're now in America." She looked different since I last saw her. Apart from the obvious not being dead aspect, this Freida looked subtly improved. Her breasts were a lot smaller but a more interesting, less watermelon-like shape. Perhaps the dual detonations of her previous implants had made her think twice about returning to her prior gargantuan cleavage. Explosively high volume tits clearly had their drawbacks.

"You're looking much better than the last time we met." I

commented, taking the pressure off Freida's stomach and sitting back into a squat.

"Yes, thank heavens for nano-surgery." Although Freida had been ripped to shreds by the attack at my house, she hadn't been killed immediately, which was all she needed to survive. For a number of years, she explained, her bloodstream had contained illegal experimental nano-surgeons that lay dormant until they sensed the host organism was in mortal danger. They then jumped into action to keep the injured host alive. But the nano-surgeons I knew of just kept you in a stable, liveable condition. They didn't rebuild you into a fashionable new body style, ready to travel across the Atlantic just a few hours later. Freida clearly had access to some radical, new and exceptionally powerful nano-medicine.

I stood up and looked around. Nobody was taking a blind bit of notice that I'd just wrestled someone to the floor in broad daylight. They were all just going about their business, or lack thereof, with scant attention to what anybody else was doing. You'd have needed to drive a vehicle right into Washington Square Park and run a few people over to pique anyone's interest. This had actually happened a few decades previously. The lack of attention was probably also how Michelle had managed to disappear in the few seconds I'd been concentrating on pinning Freida down in her aluminium baking wrap.

Michelle was nowhere to be seen. She'd either run off, been abducted by a drug addict, or been grabbed by whoever it was that thought she was "the One". The latter seemed most plausible, purely because it was so implausible that anyone would cotton onto my Maud Bristol ruse without good reason. This was clearly part of the grand conspiracy against me that it was fast becoming my life's work to escape.

"Any idea where my friend went?" I asked Freida as she struggled to her feet.

"You mean that little poppet you had following you around?" replied Freida coyly.

"I don't remember me having any other companion," I countered, flippantly.

"Oh, a couple of guys grabbed her and bundled her into a black car while you were having your little tussle with me," continued Freida, in an annoyingly offhand manner. "You know, we really should find a hotel somewhere and have a more personal tussle that's a bit more ecstatic. I rather enjoyed being manhandled to the floor by you. I guess some feelings never change, however much surgery you have."

"I have this great apartment in Soho we could check out." I suggested, thinking I could lure Freida down to the place I'd uncovered during my Gore Library research, then tie her up and leave her there. "It would be a bit of a hike, but I think you'll appreciate the location." If I played along with her, I reckoned it would save me the hassle of having to dispose of her in broad daylight. I'd also get the opportunity to find out if she knew anything about Michelle's disappearance. Freida seemed to like my suggestion of heading to the apartment, so I hailed a cab and we headed south.

Log 000011010111 – Machines that understand language bridge the gap between thought and action. But if they can both think and act, are these machines not more alive than humankind itself, and more powerful? Their deeds are their thoughts, and their thoughts are their deeds. Human weakness comes from the uncertainty over where brains and bodies meet.

I paid our Inuit taxi driver and we headed down Mercer Street towards the loft. During the journey I'd ascertained from Freida that Michelle had been kidnapped by Freida's friends at the League of Future Life. She was fairly open about it. Freida herself was merely enlisted to distract my attention while they grabbed Michelle. Apparently, the Monsignor medical company had been performing research on Michelle that was of particular interest to the League, so they thought she could be useful to them. Not only that, but one of the Mind Invasion victims had also been in charge of the very lab Michelle had escaped from. Silly me - I'd been sitting on a big clue and I hadn't even realised it. Blind luck had led me to her, and sheer blindness had stopped me from taking advantage of the situation. A few days previously I had even analysed some of the data from Roger Smyth, the Monsignor doctor who'd been kidnapped in one of the Mind Invasion cases. But when Michelle told me her story a few hours previously I'd failed to make the connection. I was too wrapped up in my own quest for the Pure Light Abacus and had lost sight of the Mind Invasions.

"So you also sent that note saying she was 'the one', then?" I asked. Freida looked genuinely nonplussed.

"I don't think so," she confirmed. "What message was that? One of what?" Freida was a bad actor, and she clearly wasn't even trying to fool me here. She genuinely didn't know anything about that note. This meant either that someone else in the League had sent it and hadn't told her about it, or that yet another party was involved. Considering the devout following of interested organisations I had started collecting, it could have been any one of a number of bizarre groups. Maybe it was the Chinese.

I asked Freida where the League were planning to take Michelle, and explained that I would be retrieving her at all costs. Unfortunately, the League had the right attitude about Freida and hadn't told her what they were intending to do with Michelle. They knew full well that trusting Freida with any valuable information was like getting a hungry crocodile to baby-sit your new born child. So I was going to have to track down Michelle myself. For some reason, it aggravated me to think of Michelle being poked and tested by League of Future Life goons. Michelle didn't seem to deserve the hard life she was having, and I felt responsible for landing her back amongst people who only wanted her for their scientific experiments. Then again, I'd temporarily saved her from a life amongst people who only wanted her for their sexual experiments. Either way, finding her again would have to wait. Freida and I had arrived at the door of the Soho loft from within which the Andorran conflagration had been triggered, and it was time to investigate.

I inspected the twin buzzers for the two apartments in the building looking for the key-card slot. The door had no obvious electronic fastening mechanism. Instead, an antique mechanical lock from the Twentieth century secured the latch on the door itself. At least, it would have done if the door hadn't been slightly ajar already. Unholstering my trusty flechette pistol, I cautiously pushed the portal open further. I was ready to jump aside at any moment and let Freida's brand new cleavage take the brunt of any gunfire, but none came. We entered the hall and slowly climbed the stairs, in safety. Nobody challenged us. The top floor apartment was the one pinpointed by my tracing software, and its door was also slightly ajar. I motioned for Freida to wait quietly outside. Then I burst into the room while executing a forward roll that would have made any Hong Kong action movie director proud, although I only had one gun.

There wasn't anybody there, just a whole load of computer equipment. Not simply one or two powerful workstations, but four full size racks of servers packed one side of the huge, high-ceilinged space. Their yellow lights flashed enigmatically as they continued their tasks, oblivious to my entrance. I quickly searched round the various partitioned spaces within the loft, my gun still drawn, then called Freida in once I knew there were no lethal surprises in store.

"Nice place you've got here," exclaimed Freida. "Kind of 1950s New York art scene meets geekdom. I do love the throb of big iron." She smiled at me. "So where's the bedroom?" I realised I'd have to make an effort at keeping up the pretence, so I led Freida over to a quarter of the loft that I'd noticed was thinly partitioned off into what passed for a bedroom. Inside, there was a huge iron four-poster bed against the one solid wall, to the right of an equally huge stained glass window depicting Bill Gates.

"The Almighty is watching," I quipped. "Do you think we should perform in His presence?"

"Oh yes," exclaimed Freida, grabbing the top of my trousers and pulling me to her. "I fully intend to monopolise the operations of your system in homage," she added. I resigned myself and got on with it. Well, resigned is perhaps too harsh a word – Freida had loads of energy, and could be quite entertaining in bed. But there was work to do, and this was an unwanted delay – and a relatively lengthy one, too.

After we'd finished, Freida sat up in bed, sucking on a cigarette in a rather clichéd fashion, except this cigarette was smokeless. I got up and stretched my back, which was aching. Just under an hour had passed and I was sore in more places than not. I wandered around the loft in my boxer shorts, my manhood strangely pleased to have a few moments of rest. Pausing by the racks of servers, I flipped on the monitor to see what the computers were all so busy doing. Cubic graphs filled the screen, with data peaking colourfully across the axes. The server farm was chewing away at some heavy algorithmic analysis. I scanned the screen more closely, letting out a sigh of exasperation when I saw the logo – it was the insignia of

SAL, the Search for Alien Life. This shared computing experience had been running on computers around the world for decades, analysing the data picked up by radio telescopes around the planet and at strategic locations in the Solar system. Algorithms were used that were similar to those created by cryptographers to detect significant linguistic structures in the jumble of seemingly random noise of an encrypted message. In SAL's case, there was no need to translate or decode the language, just detect that the expected weightings of a linguistic structure were there.

I reached for the antiquated cursor pointing device that sat on a shelf amongst the servers. A split second before my hand touched the mouse, a message flashed on the screen.

CONGRATULATIONS
YOU HAVE FOUND ALIEN LIFE
TO LEARN MORE CLICK HERE > @

Not being one to turn up the chance of meeting new and exciting friends from foreign lands, I clicked. The graphs melted away in what looked like a rather cheesy MTV music video effect. A classic 1950s flying saucer swooped from the distance into the foreground, then spurted clouds of steam while effecting a landing. A walkway slid out from the undercarriage, and an archetypal skinny grey alien with gleaming red eyes padded down. The alien waddled forward until only its head and shoulders were on screen. It stopped and proffered a hand.

"I come in peace," it said, in a voice strangely reminiscent of turn of the 21st century comic film star Jim Carey. Then it broke into a huge grin. "Who am I kidding? I come in jest! Thanks very much for the girl. You gave us just what we wanted. Now fuck off before I use my ray gun on you." Seemingly from nowhere, the little alien pulled a massive, Flash Gordon-style weapon and pointed it at me. "Bang!" said the alien, and then laughed like a Warner Brothers cartoon character, turning to prance maniacally back into its spaceship, which quickly flew into the distance. The screen then filled with flying toasters shooting fountains of lime green pop tarts.

This would all have been quite funny, had I found it humorous in any way. Instead, I was dinstinctly annoyed. I was getting more and more indignant that I'd let Michelle go so easily. It wasn't just a pride thing. Even though I hadn't really had much chance to get to know her, there was something resilient about that girl which I liked. She seemed to be someone always making her way out of trouble, rather like me. The big difference was that I looked for trouble, and she'd been born into it. I relished flying close to the sun, loving the risk of each cheeky little crime, every risqué comment that would expose the truth everyone was thinking but nobody had the guts to speak. Getting away with it was my pleasure sublime. Someone like Freida was a survivor, too, but she was also a loser. You never really wanted to work with her on a job – she'd always do something that would mess it all up. Freida always scraped through, but never with flying colours. I was very nervous about having her around.

There was a buzz at the door. I paused for a second, then retrieved my gun from the bedroom and peered at the entry videophone. Two small weasel-like men were standing at the door. One of them pushed the buzzer again. I pressed the intercom and spoke.

"Yeah? 'sup?" I inquired, faking a slight American accent. My impression was as transparent as a politician's alibi.

"We're here to make a deal, Mr Dean. For the girl. Hand over the girl and we'll make it very worth your while." It was the taller of the weasels speaking, in a fittingly nasal voice. He wore black leather gloves and a raincoat, which must have been uncomfortable in the warm weather.

"Okay," I replied, and buzzed them in. Finally my chance to make some money out of Freida had come. As the two skinny rodent-men shuffled into the loft I added, "so how much are you going to give me for her?"

"That depends on what condition she's in," said the taller weasel, obviously the leader of the duo. I motioned for them to follow me towards the sleeping area. There we found Freida sprawled face down on the bed, a paisley-patterned sheet half covering her surgically crafted posterior. She had dozed off after her cigarette.

"So where's the girl?" asked weasel number one, eying my boxer shorts with some suspicion. I knew they couldn't really have meant Freida. Using the word girl was a dead giveaway in itself. The idea that anyone would want to pay to take Freida away with them was also thoroughly laughable. But you could always hope. I turned towards the weasels with a mock quizzical frown, which I executed with far better aplomb than my American accent.

"Who do you mean then? This is the only girl here." I gesticulated around the loft with the gun I was still holding. The smaller weasel made a rather pathetic attempt to put his hand behind his back for a weapon that was clearly secured under his belt there. I pointed mine very clearly at him. "Move any more at all and I will kill you both, very quickly but very messily. And that includes breathing. And blinking." Weasel number two froze so immediately it took all my concentration not to laugh. "Okay, I know who you're really after but I'm afraid she's not here. I'd love to take your money as part of whatever slave trading business you're into, but I don't have the goods you want. She ran away from me a few hours ago in Washington Square. Your guess is as good as mine where she's gone."

Studying the rather unfashionable attire of the two men, I noticed both were wearing pins on their lapels depicting cute-looking panda bears. Far from being a symbol that they were members of an international wildlife conservation organisation, this was a company logo - the Monsignor medical company's logo. Monsignor had pioneered the commercialisation of cloning, but had met with fierce opposition from moralists and environmentalists. In a brilliant PR move, the company had offered to clone the last remaining male giant panda, which had failed over many years to mate successfully with the last female, causing a crisis when the last female panda died. Monsignor genetically engineered both female and male giant pandas en masse, saving the specie from extinction. At the same time, Monsignor subtly altered the giant panda's taste in food so that it would no longer eat only young bamboo shoots. Now the lovable black and white bear would hungrily consume grass, most vegetables, and even cooked meat. It was particularly partial to cheeseburgers. As a result, pandas had become popular as pets, and you'd often see them out for a stroll with their owners in the park. In China they were so prevalent that they'd become a pest, and an annual panda cull had to be instigated.

Clearly, the two weasels had been employed by Monsignor to retrieve Michelle, and they'd come pretty close. This was worrying. Everyone seemed to know my whereabouts before even I myself had decided to go there. Mind you, information had become more valuable than gold. I asked the tall weasel how he'd found me, and he explained that they'd recently traced Michelle to Kings Cross through a policeman she'd had as a client. Then I stepped in and spoiled their plans to capture her. Fortunately, they'd had an anonymous tip-off about where I was to be found a few hours earlier, and they'd got to New York as fast as they could. Too late again, but at least they were still probably in the right city to find Michelle.

The taller man looked momentarily at the shorter, and then mumbled something about how if I didn't have what they were looking for then they'd be going. The pair appeared more like bureaucrats than hired killers. I didn't fancy their chances of retrieving Michelle from the League of Future Life. I didn't fancy mine, either, but at least I could handle myself in a fight. These guys looked as if their panda bear mascot would have given them a hard time even if they were allowed to throw the first punch. The duo shuffled out of the loft and into the sunny Manhattan afternoon, and that was to be the last I saw of them alive.

Surprisingly, Freida had slept through the whole thing. Her mouth was slightly open and she was making little snuffling noises as if she was in the depths of an emotional dream. I pondered whether to leave her in the loft or wake her up and take her with me. I also considered tying her up and brutalising her with unspeakable violence - maybe stuffing something intended as a cooking implement into that gaping mouth. But just as a really devilish and obscene plan formulated in my mind, Freida awoke, yawned, stretched and grabbed me. She was rested and up for more. I excused myself, explaining that I was ravenously hungry, which was actually true, and wanted to go out to a cafe to grab something to eat, which wasn't. In fact I'd decided to head to Brooklyn. I wanted to visit an old hacker artist friend who might be able to help me trace what was going on with the animated alien, and perhaps find who it was that always seemed one step ahead of me. I also hadn't seen him in ages and fancied swapping a few tales.

Log 000011010111 – Great power presents great opportunity for humour. The profoundest understanding comes with seeing the ludicrousness in our existence.

I studied the menus outside some of the trendiest Soho coffee and cake shops, then wrinkled my nose in disdain as if nothing in the neighbourhood took my fancy. I suggested that we head to a cafe I knew in Williamsburg in Brooklyn. Williamsburg was an area that had gone from up and coming artist habitat, through chic and expensive, to its present state of decline. It still had a few top quality hangouts from its highly fashionable era, but I didn't actually remember the names of any of them. So I told Freida that we were going to the New York branch of London's famous Amalfi on Old Compton Street, still going strong since the Twentieth Century. I was pretty sure she didn't know New York well enough to realise I was blatantly lying, but I knew she liked to frequent the Amalfi in London. She took to the idea of an Amalfi in Brooklyn with some enthusiasm. Freida liked cake and coffee with steamed milk, especially when served to her table by camp Italians wearing ill-fitting wigs.

The taxi headed for the Williamsburg bridge. Freida was nattering about something and I was gazing out at the people on the sidewalk. An extremely tall, skinny woman was wandering down Delancey Street wearing a short tight-fitting dress made of light-emitting polymer. The dress appeared to be one big flexible video screen, showing slowly evolving fractal patterns, except on the posterior where two talking heads – one on each buttock – faced each-other and were having a conversation. The woman had a talk show broadcasting on her ass. As our taxi drove past, I realised the woman was actually a man, with the control equipment for the dress in his/her false breasts. This transvestite was one of the famous Manhattan Prime Time Queens, a little far east from his/her regular Greenwich Village habitat. The Prime Time Queens were world renown for their drag costumes that always incorporated viewing screens of some sort showing classic TV shows of the 1990s, such as Jerry Springer. This particular Queen was clearly rich and able to afford the most technologically advanced wraparound attire.

We continued along Delancey and mounted the top carriageway of the bridge. Arriving in Williamsburg a minute or so later felt like entering a different city entirely. My friend Gino's apartment was in a new industrial area in a part of Williamsburg that had gone full circle. Abandoned studios and loft apartments were being regenerated into warehouses and business units. Gino lived opposite a garage where stolen cars were cut into easily-sold, untraceable parts. A fenced courtyard adjacent to his building was patrolled by huge genetically-enhanced cyborg dogs wearing bullet-proof waistcoats and canine helmets. The neighbourhood was virtually deserted, even during the day. Only a few years previously the streets would have been alive with fashionable people, but the great and the good had moved on to a different up and coming part of the city. I paid the Bolivian taxi driver and we sauntered towards the dilapidated, paint-peeling door to Gino's building. Freida was frowning. She was on the verge of figuring out that I was lying about the Amalfi cafe. I delayed the inevitable by telling her that we'd be going there after I'd picked something up from a friend.

Gino buzzed us into the entrance hall and we climbed the tight flights of stairs to his door. The building had no passenger elevator - it had been considered chic to do without such modernist amenities when the original factory shell was renovated into apartments. Residents soon realised this was an error when they moved in, but the ones who'd lived there since it was an artist hangout refused to consider the upgrade. To them the lack of an elevator meant more than a retro fashion statement - it meant less outside interference. Without an elevator, the building automatically repelled the most shallow of the fashion victims. Gino was one of the first people to rent a place in this building, and he'd probably be the last, moving out only when his apartment was overrun by gang bangers wielding portable artillery. For now the area was still safe enough, at least once you got inside your home.

A sullen girl in her late teens or early twenties wearing only a loose vest and panties closed the door behind us and secured the dead bolt. She padded back down the hall without a word. I set off after her with Freida close behind. The girl pointed a finger through a door at the end of the passage, and then disappeared through another door opposite. We walked from the hall into a huge space with cavernous ceilings. It appeared to be two stories high. Inside, reclining on the largest bean bag I'd ever seen, was Gino. He was at least ten years older than me, and virtually bald, but a strict fitness regime involving the teaching of acrobaerobics had preserved an impressive physique. Acrobaerobics was the latest exercise fad – high impact aerobics based around circus acrobat training. The trendiest gyms were now equipped with trapezes, high wires, trampolines and unicycles, so gym members could train in circus performance whilst simultaneously keeping fit._Gino had been teaching it for years before it was fashionable, as a sideline to pay for his artistic endeavours. Even now that his digital art was world-famous, Gino still taught acrobaerobics, but mostly for the purpose of meeting physically fit young women.

As I walked over to Gino's beanbag he leapt up to embrace me. I explained that Freida and I were stopping by on our way to Amalfi, with a little wink. We'd always had a rapport, almost like twin brothers. He proceeded to offer us his own cake and beverages, explaining that he was after all of Italian-American extraction and that fancy pastries and coffee were his stock in trade. "I hear Amalfi is not what it used to be! Stay here with me!" insisted Gino. I glanced at Freida, who gave me an indignant look, then shrugged acquiescence. Gino walked into the hall for a second and called out for coffee and cake to the girl, whose name appeared to be Suzanna. With a scowl, Suzanna skulked off to a corner of the huge space, where a classic 1950s-style fridge stood next to a work surface bearing various intriguing culinary gadgets. Banging coffee cups and containers onto the table as if they were personally responsible for her foul mood, Suzanna prepared our drinks and pastries.

A few minutes later, we sat drinking freshly-brewed Columbian roast and nibbling creamy puffed confections. I asked Gino what he knew about project Pure Light Abacus. He smiled coyly, as if I'd requested information about the whereabouts of Bigfoot or some other phenomenon that only a fool might think really existed. As it turned out, he wasn't really laughing at me so much as with me.

"Well, it's a really powerful supercomputer for one thing," he began. "I saw on the news this morning that it was stolen from a laboratory in Europe a few days ago. I immediately thought of you, Bentley. Not many people are foolhardy enough to steal something as high profile as that." Gino went on to talk about how he'd heard that the Pure Light Abacus had been exhibiting some very strange behaviour leading up to its disappearance.

Gino created art based around algorithms. He'd designed a series of digital frames containing constantly changing patterns. These were derived from equations such that they would never looked the same from one moment to the next. He knew quite a bit about artificial intelligence, so he'd been keeping an eye on Project Pure Light Abacus for years, because it was exponentially more powerful than any computer that had gone before. Given the right seed algorithms, it had the potential to behave unpredictably enough to seem like a living being. But he'd heard the machine had recently been malfunctioning, providing bizarrely inaccurate results to equations that were straight logic. Nevertheless, it was still the most powerful computing platform around in terms of raw horsepower and lots of people wanted it. Some of the scientists involved had been kidnapped. One religious group even believed the Pure Light Abacus was God descended to Earth, and had started a bombing campaign. They were insisting the Abacus be moved to the Church of the Holy Sepulchre in Jerusalem. Without boring him with the gory details, I told Gino about how I was doing research into the kidnapped Pure Light Abacus scientists.

"I was following a data trace from the Pure Light Abacus's Andorran home and it led to a loft apartment in New York," I explained. "That was where I found this really cute little alien animation." As he was an animation expert, I thought perhaps Gino would have a suggestion about its origin. He smiled that same coy smile, as if I'd said something stupid again. He reached under the glass coffee table to the shelf beneath and pulled out a sales pamphlet. In an era of networked communications, you could still find yourself flooded with paper circulars, albeit smart paper with extensive interactive multimedia capabilities. Flinging the pamphlet into the space in front of me like a croupier dealing a card, Gino asked, "Did it look anything like that?"

I looked down. On the front cover of the pamphlet was a little grey alien exactly the same as the one in Soho. It drew a ray gun from a hip holster, pointed it and winked. Over and over again, the animation replayed, and luminous green lettering flashed along the top:

SEEING THINGS? THEN YOU NEED A HOLIDAY!
TRY A CRYOGENIC SABBATICAL FROM VEGAS VACATIONS.
IT'S OUT OF THIS WORLD!

My heart pounded fast for a second or so as a mini-explosion of associations detonated inside my head.

"This is just a little too much of a coincidence, Gino," I commented finally. "I feel like someone's leaving me really stupid clues. You're not in on it too, are you?" Gino smiled coyly again. For a second I thought he was the one leaving me the clues, but that was a little too paranoid - Gino was an old friend. I picked up the alien pamphlet and browsed. As the name suggested, Vegas Vacations was based in Las Vegas, Nevada, but the company had facilities around the globe, including London. It was the leading maker of cryogenic holiday homes, supplying units to the rich and famous. The idea that Vegas Vacations could be the organisation behind the mind invasions seemed far too obvious to be likely. In fact, it had been the first place investigators had looked, and there was no evidence of direct involvement. But there was clearly a link of some kind, even if the company itself wasn't culpable.

Just as I'd reached a point in my thinking where I was truly confused, loud and repeated swearing came from the kitchen area. Sullen Suzanna had managed to stab herself quite badly in the hand, whilst attempting to separate the two halves of a frozen bagel with a French professional chef's kitchen knife,. Her blood was dribbling all over the chrome sink. Gino, with a sigh, raised himself from his beanbag and sauntered towards her.

"You've always had problems dealing with bread products, haven't you Suze?" he chuckled. "Good thing it wasn't a focaccia. At least you can trust a good Jewish roll to show you some mercy. You've still got all your fingers!"

Although Suzanna's injury was unlikely to be life-threatening, Gino was going to have to take her for professional treatment. I gulped down the last dregs of my coffee and suggested Freida and I leave. Gino said he could drop us on the way to the hospital at a place where we'd be more likely to find a cab. We ended up at Grand Army plaza. As I wirelessly hailed a passing taxi, an idea struck me. I turned to Freida.

"Ever been married?" I asked. Freida shook her head, her eyes sparkling with interest. So I suggested we head off to Vegas.

Log 000011010111 – If a lion could speak, we wouldn't understand it. If we met aliens, maybe we wouldn't have enough in common with them to realise what they were saying. Perhaps we have already met aliens, but didn't even notice they were there.

I'd given up on finding Michelle for the time being. Although I wanted to track her down, I didn't have any leads in New York. She would almost certainly have been taken out of the city soon after capture. At least, that's what I would have done. But something told me that if I got to the root of the mind invasions and found the Pure Light Abacus, I'd find Michelle again. Visiting Vegas Vacations felt like a trap but there was nothing left to do except to keep moving, and I was arrogant enough to think I could deal with whatever situation I found myself in. After all, I'd escaped from quite a few hazardous scrapes recently. I was beginning to enjoy this life on the move. It was a bit like taking a tourist package trip, except that the complimentary holiday activities consisted of gun battles and assorted violent encounters around every corner.

Las Vegas had clusters of skycar parking lots around the outskirts of the city. From there you could take terrestrial taxis or the monorail into the old town or the strip. Twenty years previously, the whole of the Las Vegas metropolitan area had been encased in a huge biosphere, making the entire conurbation fully climate controlled, once and for all ending the distinction between night and day. As soon as you got out of your vehicle at a skycar lot, you knew you were entering a completely man-made world of gambling and sensationalist entertainment. At each lot, a moving walkway embedded with virtual poker machines took you to the taxi rank or monorail. Some of the less well-off never even bothered to go any further. They flew in from around the country and got onto one of these walkways, which went around in huge meandering circles and featured constantly changing holographic entertainment as a backdrop. You could simply stand on one with your family and your small credits and play the virtual poker until your money dried up. You could then jump straight back into your vehicle and head home. For the hopeless white trash gambler, it was a one stop shop to rid yourself of any excess money that might have been needlessly wasted on your children's education.

During the flight from New York, I had tried to sleep. But it was hard to take a nap with someone like Freida in the next seat. Before allowing myself to rest, I'd manufactured myself a reason and an identity with which to visit Vegas Vacations. Then I'd securely locked out every control or computerised console available in the skycar, even those stitched into my DKNY leisurewear. I'd have been a fool to trust Freida Eglin, even if she was excited by the prospect of marrying me. I'd told her that we would take a cryogenic sabbatical as a honeymoon, so I didn't have to explain to her why I wanted to go to Vegas Vacations. After I'd parked the skycar, Freida was annoyingly excited as we jumped onto the moving walkway. She grabbed the nearest virtual poker machine and managed to blow 15,000 euros in the five minutes it took us to get to the monorail. Fortunately, 15,000 euros could buy you scarcely more than a bargain meal in a fast food restaurant.

I'd booked us into the Hotel Caligula. It seemed appropriate considering the constant mayhem that had become my life. The Caligula was an "X Hotel", which was a Vegas term for a boarding establishment that did not admit anyone below the age of 21. The free entertainment in the gambling hall of an X Hotel could legally be a lot more raunchy than in family accommodation. As Frieda and I strolled through the foyer of the Caligula, around us bio-engineered robot actors portrayed scenes from the Roman emperor's biography. A small crowd of day trippers and visitors from other hotels was huddled around a raised dais. Atop the dais, lifelike animatronic mannequins were re-enacting the infamous moment when the mad emperor had personally performed a caesarean section on one of his concubines. Blood was flying all over the stage, but the crimson fountain was designed not to reach the audience. The Caligula robot's face grinned maniacally as he extracted the struggling baby. The show was enacted every hour, and was one of the attractions the hotel offered to entice gamblers to its virtual poker machines and magneto-roulette. Las Vegas was the home of over-the-top entertainment. Other hotels had lions on Prozac lying right next to the blackjack tables, but the Caligula had obscenely graphic spectacles of Roman debauchery instead. It wasn't pleasant but it kept the punters coming back.

I'd managed to secure the Senator Suite, which had an equine theme to commemorate Caligula making his favourite horse a senator. From our hotel room I ordered the delivery of some new clothes. I'd been wearing the same DKNY outfit for a couple of days by then, and although I'd washed it at Michelle's it had been through a lot. I needed a change. Freida had leapt straight onto the huge king-size bed and made seductive eyes at me, until she realised I was preoccupied with my quest for fresh, fashionable attire. With a piqued look she snatched the remote control off the bedside table and searched for something to watch. On more than one channel, the holographic entertainment system was broadcasting a political message from the US president. The elected American leader at that time was an animated 3D figurine. The cartoon premier was named Dr Kennedy and was controlled by committee. Two years previously the youthful-looking graphic had swept to power as an independent candidate, gaining a full ten per cent more votes than the Republican and Democratic candidates combined. Political pundits surmised the American people were embracing the high tech future and a new form of politics. The more cynical argued that the real reason was Dr Kennedy's solid platform pledging that guns would be kept legal, abortion wouldn't, and a foreign country would be bombed every two years.

My clothes were soon delivered by a robotic bell boy, a black and white trolley with its own independent computerised personality. It was programmed to transport room service items and engage in simple small talk. A generous tip was automatically added to your hotel bill at every possible opportunity. The bell boy also brought food – a Philly cheese steak for me and a Caligula special chicken liver salad with cream dressing for Freida. I ate and then showered. I was finally ready to investigate Vegas Vacations. Freida wanted to come with me, but I explained that I wanted the wedding venue and honeymoon to be a surprise. Little did she know what I meant by "surprise".

The clothes I'd purchased were by Japanese designer Sammy Kyoto, an up and coming stylist of prêt a porter urban cyberwear. I donned the snappy single-breasted suit, which was made of a special kind of laminated paper. It was smart and efficient-looking, had pockets everywhere for all my important gadgets, and incorporated concealed power conduits. You could route electricity and optical data throughout the fabric. The suit wasn't just functional, it was blue and shiny and looked great. But there was a design flaw I hadn't realised from the product description - the outfit rustled. I wasn't going to be able to sneak up on anyone whilst wearing this getup, unless they were extremely hard of hearing or happened to be loitering in a paper bag factory. I didn't want to wait around for more clothing, so I had to make do with the Kyoto. At least I looked the part of the successful British hairdresser I was about to impersonate. That was the cover I'd invented to take me into Vegas Vacations. I didn't really care if my ruse only lasted a few minutes, so long as it got me past the front door. Once I was inside, I'd have a chance to look around.

Vegas Vacations had its head office on the strip, not far from the New Luxor Hotel. The office building was in the form of a stylised gothic castle planted on a small manmade mountaintop. Within the fully controlled Las Vegas climate, the castle was kept in perpetual night. A thunderstorm frowned overhead, straight out of a classic B-grade vampire movie. Forked lightning flashed down to the tallest spire every few seconds, lighting the entire building. Thunder rumbled, although no rain was falling. A torrential deluge would have been authentic, but would also have annoyed visiting clients. Rain control was only triggered when the vegetation needed watering, and only then locally to the plants.

The taxi pulled up in front of the huge wooden doors that marked the foyer of Vegas Vacations, and I stepped out alone. I'd left Freida gambling at the Caligula with a pile of my money. At least it would keep her busy, even if it wasn't good for my bank balance. Once I'd made my way inside the Vegas Vacations castle, the outer appearance was immediately revealed for what it was – a theatrical front hiding a cutting edge high tech business. Past the huge doors was a massive vestibule six stories high, with an enormous embalmed palm tree in each corner. Twin banks of three glass elevators each were scurrying up and down the far wall, their occupants visible inside. The hall was subdivided by a security barrier that separated the front entrance from the lifts and doorways beyond.

I sauntered up to the central reception desk and introduced myself as Keith Windsor, London hairdresser to the rich and famous. Every one of the receptionists was anatomically perfect and immaculately made up, all of which was spoilt by their huge sculpted hairdos resembling cresting waves. I'd chosen a blonde with silvery brown lipstick. Her nasal accent picked her out as a native of suburban New York. She smiled in a way that seemed focused on a point a good few miles past me, as if she were talking to somebody in the far distance. The effect was most unnerving, but I ignored it and explained I had an appointment with a sales executive to discuss the purchase of a personal cryogenic sabbatical unit for my salon, and possibly a deluxe programme for myself on-site as a taster. I'd booked the appointment on the way to Vegas. The sales rep I'd been allotted was named Norman Sadler. He was currently not at his desk, but I was half an hour early so this wasn't a problem. The receptionist motioned to some very comfortable-looking leather media armchairs and I sat down to wait. The media chairs had a fully immersive entertainment system built into each one, to keep customers happy while they awaited service.

I wasn't planning to use the entertainment system, though I'd deliberately come early in order to give myself an excuse for watching people come and go through the Vegas Vacations lobby. I wanted to observe who was visiting, and look for holes in the security. I'd been lolling in the exquisite leather armchair for about twenty minutes when someone walked through the lobby whose face seemed familiar. But I couldn't quite place him. He looked like somebody I'd met recently, but with a distinct difference that I was unable to put my finger on. He walked up to the desk and passed something to the same blonde receptionist I'd spoken to. She looked at it and then smiled directly at him rather than miles into the distance, finally motioning for him to go through the security barrier. This was a simple chrome gate, but I was sure it would be backed up with automated immobilisers, designed to incapacitate forced entrants within the legally allowed boundaries of pain. Searching the walls and ceilings for emplacements, I finally realised that the very exotic-looking plants strategically placed in pots and hanging baskets were in fact the security arrangements. Their curiously shaped flowers concealed automatic gun emplacements.

Five minutes more passed and finally a skinny man in a classic pinstripe suite emerged from one of the glass elevators and walked purposefully towards me. He didn't need to stop at the reception to check who I was. He already knew. The chrome gate swung open for him without his touching it as he strode through with his right arm outstretched.

"Keith, I'm Norman. Welcome to Vegas Vacations!" He beamed. I rose from my chair, my paper suit rustling audibly, and shook his hand. He passed me a lapel button, motioning for me to attach it to my clothing. It adhered automatically when close to the material's surface. The chrome gate opened again as we walked through and headed towards the nearest glass elevator. Norman continued his well-rehearsed greeting patter with some facts and figures about the Vegas Vacations headquarters and other offices around the world. Apparently, 1,500 people worked in this building, which was designed by Vietnamese architect Trinh Kieu. Vegas Vacations employed 14,000 worldwide, and so on. I phased out quickly. If I'd wanted to hear corporate presentations I wouldn't have chosen a career of crime. Not that crime was paying well at the moment. In fact, it had been so long since I'd last stolen anything that I'd almost forgotten. I pledged to pilfer something valuable within the next 24 hours to keep my hand in.

Norman led me to an airy office with a screen taking up one entire wall. We sat in comfortable steel chairs either side of an exquisite mahogany boardroom table. Norman switched into his main sales pitch. Voice cues embedded in his presentation triggered motion in elements of the animated graphics that filled the wall screen. The highlighted sections illustrated his main point, which was what a cryogenic sabbatical could do for me. Cryogenic sabbatical was a trademarked blend of virtual reality entertainment, suspended animation, and dream therapy. It was very much the fashionable thing amongst those who could afford it, mainly because the machinery allowed an entire year's mental experience to be packed into just two weeks, or a day trip into less than an hour. During sabbaticals of more than a few days, the body's muscles were also automatically toned during the process. Busy executives could take a well-earned break without losing much downtime in the fast-moving world of commerce, yet still come back rested, physically fit, and much better adjusted. I decided to throw a spanner in the works, and asked Norman what he thought about the mind invasion cases I'd heard about on the news. Did he think there was a fault with Vegas Vacations equipment, and was it really safe? Norman became nervous and defensive, then started gibbering safety statistics. I listened philosophically for a minute or so, and finally asked if I could try a sabbatical before committing to purchasing a unit. I told Norman I'd feel more secure offering the service to my customers if I'd experienced it safely myself.

So Norman took me to another room a few doors down from the

presentation office. The space was smaller and more claustrophobic. Along one side was the cryogenic sabbatical booth, which looked like a cross between a sun bed and an Egyptian sarcophagus. It was a horizontal unit lit inside and was contoured to resemble a stylised human form. Unlike the conscious direction that was possible when you used ordinary virtual reality entertainment, with a cryogenic sabbatical you didn't choose how your mind got to spend its time off. The process worked in a deeper way, pulling subject matter from your subconscious to create a world of your own dreams. Some had described it as automated Freudian psychoanalysis only not as expensive. For such a complicated device, the booth's controls were simple, with most parameters set automatically by the machine itself. All the operator needed to do was adjust a simple intensity control somewhere between "mild" and "strong", and then hit the green "go" button. On the booth I was contemplating getting into, a keycard slot next to the intensity control allowed the limiting circuits to be taken offline, for those who relished a really rough ride. A disclaimer next to the slot explained that Vegas Vacations wouldn't guarantee your health under such circumstances.

After I'd examined the machinery, Norman took a little bow and motioned for me to enter the booth. I pursed my lips quizzically, and asked if there was a toilet nearby that I could use first. It was just down the hall on the left apparently. I was thinking about disappearing off round the building, although surveillance was probably everywhere. I was deep in thought about how to escape detection and which direction to head, so I wasn't really looking where I was going. Walking towards the nearby toilet, I collided with someone who also hadn't bothered to look before hurrying out of a side room. It was the man I'd thought I recognised in the lobby. He turned to glare at me, and I was surprised to see that the force of our coming together had dislocated his nose. In fact, it looked like it was about to come off.

Then I realised who I was looking at. A wig and false nose had prevented me from recognising him previously, but this was the guy from the League of Future Life who had interrogated me in London. It was No Nose. He recognised me too, and reached behind his back to pull a gun from the rear of his trousers. I hadn't brought mine – the detectors in a building like this would have picked it up in a millisecond. But No Nose was clearly allowed to carry his gun with him. It was an antique magnum, a classic that should have been in a museum, to which my paper suit would afford little resistance. I put on my most joyous grin while No Nose re-secured his fake nose, all the time keeping a watchful eye and the barrel of his gun trained upon me.

"What an incredible surprise!" I gushed.

"I can see that you're continuing your research, Mr Dean," commented No Nose. "And you have singularly failed to report in to us any findings."

"Well, er, I haven't found anything very conclusive. What is your name, by the way? We were never formally introduced."

"You don't need to know who I am. And I do know how little you've found out. We have found a lot more without you. I do thank you for leading us to the experimental subject, your little girlfriend. A lucky coincidence. She will be the vessel for the coming of Future Life."

No Nose was beginning to lose me. He was starting to babble like an acolyte of an insane religious cult - which in all probability he was. The League of Future Life had its periphery who just wanted to augment themselves illegally for sport or other personal activities. But there was also a hard core that thought they were engineering the future of the human race. No Nose sounded like one of these. What it was he thought Michelle represented and what they were going to do with her I dreaded to think. She hadn't been able to remember very much of her time at Monsignor, just nasty snippets here and there. Whatever Michelle had been bred by Monsignor to test was unclear, but it sounded like something useful for the League. I realised that my hunch about Vegas Vacations had led me in exactly the right direction, an uncanny intuition even for me.

No Nose motioned for me to enter the room he had been in the process of leaving when we bumped into each other. It was similar to the one I'd left Norman in, only larger. Three cryogenic sabbatical booths dominated one wall.

"I'm afraid it's time for you to take an extended holiday, Mr Dean. You will not enjoy your trip. It's been nice working with you. Thanks again for the girl. Now get in the booth."

"You expect me to talk?" I inquired.

"Oh no, Mr Dean, I expect you to die!" cackled No Nose.

I could think of nothing else but to do as I was told. I had none of my more useful gadgets with me for getting out of such scrapes. It seemed I'd been overconfident of my cat-like survival. Once I'd climbed into the middle booth, No Nose locked it shut. I could still see him through the glass viewing screen. He pulled a keycard out of a breast pocket. I heard the sound of the dial being twisted and a whoosh as the unit surged into life. Then I started to feel cold.

Log 000011110110 – Western society is built around the concept of the individual. But individuals build up their personalities by identifying with the people around them and those they experience through the media. So an individual is in fact a blend of other people's individualities. So what, if anything, makes each person special?

My vision was filled with green lights, flashing and dancing in cryptic patterns. In their midst was a beautiful girl who looked like Michelle. I was dancing too. My feet weren't touching the floor because there was no floor. The ice cream I was eating was delicious - rich and thick with real pieces of cherry in it. The clothes I was wearing were exquisite. They were pink and fitted perfectly, with just enough give round the joints for comfort. They were my skin.

I could see for miles. The stars stretched out and I could look past them and beyond. I was lying in the long grass of a sunny field. A beautiful girl lay beside me, giggling. Her large, fertile breasts shivered as she laughed. She looked mischievous. I rolled onto her. The girl's laughing sounded like it was outside the house, or I had cotton wool in my ears. The house was more of a mansion, with an enormous wooden staircase leading up to a grand balcony. I was happy to live there with my wife, Sally. Now that the children were grown up, I could spend more time on my hobby of mountain climbing. The cliff was sheer and there was a slight wind, but I found it easy to grab each new handhold as Jon and I made our way up to the summit. I turned to survey the view across the alien planet. My hand slipped and I lost my footing. Futilely, I flailed at the cliff as it flew past me. Then I was plummeting through a void. I fell for hours, days, perhaps even weeks.

I opened my eyes and had to close them again immediately because the light was too bright. It made my retinas burn. I was seized by an uncontrollable coughing fit. Slowly I prised my lids ajar, getting accustomed to the light again. At last I could see. The cryogenic sabbatical booth was open and I was still lying prostrate in it, feeling too weak to move. Someone was standing over me, hands on hips, but my eyes were still smarting too much for me to make out who it was. Slowly my vision came into focus. The person above me was Freida, and she was alone. She grinned and bent over to examine me more closely. I could smell her powerful fruity perfume, which always hit you like a baseball bat in the gonads, and if you were unlucky this was often followed by a real baseball bat in the gonads wielded by Freida's own skinny yet powerful arms. In this instance, she seemed truly sympathetic.

"Bentley? Are you okay?" she cooed. "That naughty Albert put this sun bed on full with no safety limit! I think he was trying to annoy you." A mild annoyance would have been rather an understatement. Too long under the full rigors of cryogenic sabbatical can turn your brain to gravy. "He did the same thing to these other two," she continued, motioning to the remaining pair of booths in the room. Shivering, I lifted myself up from the reclined position and staggered to my feet. On a moderate setting, the sabbatical booth could leave you ready to leap up and face anything. On maximum for an extended period, you'd have been lucky to walk again. On the other hand, a good shake up had been known to help sufferers of Parkinson's and Alzheimer's. I wasn't in that category, although at that moment I felt like I was. It took all my concentration not to fall over. It was like being hopelessly drunk. After a minute or so of steadying myself against a wall, I regained enough bodily control to hobble over and look inside the other two booths. Staring out dopily were the two Monsignor agents I'd met in New York. Shaking, I turned off the nearest booth and stood back as the hatch swung open with an almost imperceptible whoosh – the sign of a high class piece of machinery. The man inside had obviously been there for a lot longer than I had. He was probably brain dead, and if he wasn't he might as well be.

I turned back to Freida. She smiled and held out her hand.

"We've got just enough time to get to the Elvis Chapel," she commented. "I ran out of money. Blackjack is just not for me. I prefer games where you can lie, like poker." In my state of doddering recovery, it took me a second or two to register that she'd used the word 'chapel'. I couldn't remember having booked any kind of religious service. Then it dawned on me. She was calling my bluff. She'd gone ahead and booked the wedding herself in my absence. I checked my watch and realised I'd been under for an hour and a half. I couldn't imagine the kind of bets she'd been placing to lose all the money I'd given her in such a short duration. She'd even had enough time spare to find and book a place for us to get married. "I got the hotel to track your taxi for me when you left. I always like to know where my fiancé is. I came here when I'd finished playing with the money. I met Albert on his way out and he told me he'd put you on to simmer – I don't think he realised we're engaged. I even found you under that silly false identity. Aren't I clever?"

I tossed up the pros and cons of being dead or being married to Freida. It was a tough choice. Death really did have its merits in comparison to a permanent nuptial arrangement with someone about as trustworthy as a hungry aligator. But in the long run, there were a lot more things I could do from the position of being alive as opposed to being dead. For example, I could narrowly avoid yet another attempt to kill me. To back out of Freida's plans at this juncture would probably not have been good for my health. It was all my fault anyway – I'd suggested the thing in the first place as a ruse to keep her around. I thought her connection to the League might come in handy, which in a way it had. I would probably have still been in the cryogenic booth otherwise. Then it occurred to me that Freida had walked right into Vegas Vacations and into this room, and I hadn't seen anyone with her. She seemed to have a similar run of the place to Albert. Perhaps the League was behind Vegas Vacations, behind the mind invasions, even behind the attack on my house and Chucky's pathetic attempt to kill me on the moon.

"Can we have a little look around here before we head out?" I asked.

"No time!" Freida replied immediately. "You need to hurry back and get into the tuxedo I got you while you were out. I hope it fits! Then we're going to the chapel, going to get married!" She sang the last bit, in a horrible pastiche of Doris Day. "Wait until you see my dress!" She enthused. I honestly could hardly contain my expectation.

"I came here because I thought a sabbatical would be a nice honeymoon for us," I lied. "I wanted to choose just the right one."

"How sweet," cooed Freida in an uncharacteristically fond tone. "But there's no rush. I have a platinum membership, honey. I take sabbaticals all the time."

Resigned to my fate, I followed Freida out the door. I was slowly regaining proper control of my body. We left Vegas Vacations and headed for the Caligula hotel, where Freida had a plum-coloured dinner suit waiting for me. Sulkily, I donned the ludicrous outfit, which was rounded off with a matching plum cummerbund and canary yellow bow tie. At least Freida had guessed the size correctly. The final insult was the pink Cadillac stretch limo she'd ordered to take us to the Elvis Chapel.

Fortunately, the ceremony wasn't as dull as I'd expected. Although the Elvis Chapel had originally been built by a Popist sect devoted to the worship of rock music legends, it was now in the hands of the Church of Zero, a nihilist religion based around a heavily post-Nietzschean set of beliefs. They were also known as Zeroastrians. The Church of Zero was popular with those embracing the new technology, including League of Future Life members. The central tenets of the faith were that universal ideals did not exist, only everyday experience. There was a heavy emphasis on self-extension using technology. In a parody of Christianity, fast food was offered as sacrament, including a mouthful of Holy Cola. The Church of Zero's idea of a wedding vow was gratifyingly Machiavellian. Instead of "till death do us part", it was more like "till circumstances lead either one of us to lose interest". Some would call the sentiments pessimistic, but they seemed wholly appropriate to what was likely to be a short conjugal arrangement for Freida and I. At least, if I had anything to do with it.

Somehow, Freida had managed to rustle up a respectable number of guests, including the croupier she'd been playing blackjack with. But there was still a section near the back of the hall that appeared to have been reserved. When the ceremony was half way through there was a click as the main chapel door opened and a group of people initially entered. I was facing the front towards the altar so didn't see who'd arrived. When I turned towards Freida for the vows, though, I took a peek out of the corner of my eye. Harry, Santada and the rest of Harry's entourage had joined the congregation and were reclining on the pews at the back of the chapel. I thought it was very nice of them to come to my wedding, especially as I hadn't actually invited them.

At the end of the service, as we were sipping champagne in the chapel reception area, Harry approached me wearing his habitually huge grin.

"Mr Dean, congratulations," he oozed, clearly amused by the whole situation. "So glad we could make it to this happiest day for you! Such a coincidence that we were in Las Vegas at the same time!" I pursed my lips and nodded in mock agreement.

"I guess we should talk, Harry," I confided. "There are a few things I've discovered I think you should know." Harry hadn't really been in Vegas by coincidence. He'd tracked me there with a transmitter that had been hidden on the Skycar. He'd called the Caligula while in transit to Vegas in his jet and ended up talking to Freida, who had of course invited him to the wedding. Now that Harry had found me again, I thought we might be mutually useful, especially as he wasn't in the habit of trying to kill me, at least not so far. This had become something quite rare, which I should cherish when I came across it. We agreed to meet later in one of the Caligula Hotel's more exclusive bars called The Senate.

* * *

I sidled into The Senate bar wearing my paper suit, a fashionable five minutes early for the appointment. Harry was already there, sitting with a massive Thai associate I'd not met before. The man mountain wore wraparound sunglasses, despite the low light of the drinking establishment. Harry had a cocktail of some sort, but his associate wasn't drinking anything, not even a soft drink. I ordered a frozen lime margarita.

"You haven't met Thun before, have you Bentley?" enquired Harry. I held out my hand to Thun, who didn't return the gesture, instead hinting recognition with the mildest nod of his head. His hands remained resting on the arms of the leather chair he was sitting in. I shrugged and turned back to Harry. After a few coy pleasantries, we knuckled down to a fairly earnest exchange of information. I explained how I'd come to Las Vegas to investigate Vegas Vacations, which had a connection with the Mind Invasions and the theft of the Pure Light Abacus. I hinted that the League of Future Life must also be involved in some way, as they'd kidnapped Michelle.

"I haven't had a chance to have a really good nose around Vegas Vacations," I added. "My cover was rather blown by meeting Albert from the League."

Harry smiled, as if I was a favourite child who'd just said something cute but stupid.

"Bentley, why not try the direct approach? This undercover strategy you're so fond of is not always the most economical way! Perhaps we should go there tonight? I have some gadgets I think you might appreciate. In fact, let's go now! We have plenty of time until dinner." Before I could say a word, Harry had called the waiter over and paid the bill. I'd scarcely finished my margarita. I explained I wanted to change my clothes, but Harry was insistent that we get going.

"No need to dress up – we won't be there long!" he exclaimed.

Outside the Caligula Hotel, Harry guided us to a stretch limousine that looked like it had been crossed with a military jeep. Holding the door open was one of Harry's employees that I had met before in Andorra: it was Darryl - the one with the Nanotech explosives who'd been manhandling Michelle. Inside the limousine, Harry and I sat facing forwards, while Darryl and Thun sat opposite. Thun had his arms crossed and was still wearing his sunglasses, despite the darkness inside the car. Darryl rested a large briefcase on his lap and eyed me suspiciously.

"We know where that little girl you had with you in Andorra is being held, by the way," commented Harry in an offhand manner. "The last time we checked, she was still in New York." So I'd been wrong – the League hadn't whisked her away immediately. I regretted not trying harder to find her. But, then, I didn't have Harry's advantage. It turned out Darryl had injected a radio-transmitting bug into Michelle while he manhandled her, just in case they needed to track my whereabouts. Various Thai Free State and Malaysian Secret Service radar posts could be used to track the implant. It was a smaller, less powerful transmitter than the model that had been planted in my Skycar.

The journey to Vegas Vacations was a short one. As we pulled up at the now closed gates, Darryl pulled out a small lapel badge for each of us from his briefcase. Harry explained that these were miniature ECM jammers, capable of rendering us invisible to all electromagnetic surveillance devices in the building. Cameras and motion sensors would no longer pick us up, although any noise we made could still be detected. Harry was upset because the US government wouldn't let his company sell the jammers in America through Radio Shack, but they were extremely popular in Russia, where they were virtually standard issue for the mafia police. We bundled out of the car and approached the gates. Thun had taken a set of primitive bolt cutters from the limo's trunk. He severed the chain on the gate with a single snip. Fortunately, Vegas Vacations' external security was performed via human labour only – there was no physical alarm on the gate. We strolled up to the main door, Thun balancing the bolt cutters over his shoulder like an axe. As the guard standing by the door spotted us and walked forward, Thun brought the bolt cutters down on the guard's head, cracking his skull open like a coconut and killing him instantly. Coolly, Thun returned the bolt cutters to his shoulder – all of this without ruffling his sunglasses. Darryl pulled a spray canister from his briefcase and motioned for us to stand back. He sprayed the corpse with glittering liquid. Smoke rose from the dead guard's body as his flesh and clothing fizzed, leaving just a few gold fillings and sundry jewellery behind. In less than 20 seconds he'd been dissolved, erased from existence. Uncharacteristically, my stomach was physically unsettled. How much more quickly could a being pass from living to nothingness? It seemed such an ignoble way to go – meaninglessly rubbed from the face of life without a trace, just because you had the unlucky shift that night.

Darryl returned his spray can of existential erasure to the briefcase, and removed a different type of Nanotech. Applying it to the huge main door, he formed the putty-like blob of miniature robots into the silhouette of a portal large enough for us to pass through. Acting like a cookie cutter, the Nanotech bit out a chunk of the door. This swung inwards on hinges which the nanobots had cleverly fashioned from some of the consumed material. After we'd stepped through, Darryl closed the specially created doorway behind us. He pressed a few buttons on a device he had dangling around his neck like a medallion, and the doorway was gone, as if it had never been there. The Nanotech lay on the floor at our feet in a ball. The vestibule was remarkably quiet, compared to the bustle I'd experienced there earlier in the day. Some companies opened their head offices 24 hours these days, in order to do business better in the global economy, but Vegas Vacations clearly wasn't one of them. This was going to make our evening raid all the easier. Where the receptionists with sculpted hair had sat earlier, now there was a solitary guard, lounging asleep with his feet up on the desk and a retro-style peaked cap pulled down over his face. Darryl reached into his briefcase for another gruesome death gadget, but I motioned for him to stop. Pulling my gun from its shoulder holster, I set the weapon to use tranquilliser darts with the autosilencer on. Then I shot the guard in the foot through the small gap in the plastic window. He flinched, but didn't have time to wake before the venom took effect. He'd be asleep for hours, by which time the dart would have dissolved without a trace into his bloodstream. We walked to the elevator, and headed down to the basement, which Harry explained was where the machine room containing the main computer systems was located. It had all been ridiculously easy so far.

Darryl called up a map of the building on his pocket assistant, then guided us to a room where he reckoned the main company databases would be accessible. This wasn't where they were actually kept – synchronised copies were maintained all over the world. But this was where Vegas Vacations head office's main data feed entered the building, so would be the best place to tap in. A solid metal door led into the room, secured with a retinal scan and keycard system. Darryl's briefcase of tricks quickly defeated the security, and we found ourselves in a surprisingly small room with a rack of computing equipment in one corner. A row of terminals plus a couple of empty desk spaces filled the longest open wall. Darryl pulled a small portable from his briefcase and handed it to me, motioning to one of the empty spaces.

The portable was the latest Taiwanese model, an Assist Portamate 8900 with the new Malaysian crystal Gigachip, running at 300 Terahertz. It had autolock networking technology, so all I had to do was turn it on and it hooked itself into the Vegas Vacations network, as well as four nearby coffee shops. I grabbed a choice selection of my favourite hacker tools off of Infonet and got to work breaking into the Vegas Vacations data centre. Half an hour later I had the run of the place. Internal security was obviously not this company's speciality. The first things I wanted to know were the true technical specifications of the cryogenic sabbatical booths. I discovered that Vegas had built in a 'back door' through which they could monitor the brain activity of occupants. It was common practice in all software and hardware products to have such backwards-flowing data links, so companies could perform as much market research on their customers as possible. You could opt out, but the clause for this was generally so hard to find most people didn't bother. The design of the booth data link was based on a VR rig, for a full pictorial view of what was going on in a Vegas vacationer's mind. It was built like this so booth operators could keep track of the mental health of booth occupants. Within the last six months, however, the company had started to be worried that there was a security hole in the back door system. There had been quite a number of suspicious malfunctions, all of them kept quiet in the news media. Personal data from booth users had ended up in the hands of a telemarketing firm selling holiday timeshares on Mars. The problem arose from the fact that booths could be monitored remotely from head office as well as locally. That meant the data feed passed through public networks, which it was meant to do in a heavily encrypted state. But someone had still managed to tap into it.

Even more worrying were the cases of data leakage from the prototypes of a new kind of booth. This new device had been commissioned by the Extropian wing of the League of Future Life, and was supposed to be top secret. The Extropians were the most extreme group within the League. They believed that humankind's destiny was to jettison the physical body entirely and become pure sentient data. The individual would cease to exist, having evolved into a blended community of minds living in a giant network of computers and digitally controlled machinery. Each individual consciousness would be everywhere at the same time, once and for all severing the outmoded necessity of existing in a fixed space and time. From then onwards, humankind would live in the ecstasy of communal oneness, as predicted by Karl Marx and Christian conceptions of heaven. The only problem was how to get out of the physical body in the first place, which was where Vegas Vacations' new cryogenic booth came in. Previously, a VR rig could make you feel like you'd left your body behind, but if your body was taken away so would you be. The escape from the real world was just an illusion.

Vegas Vacations' 'Mind Extractor', as the engineers working on the new device fondly called it, could do something much more sophisticated than a VR rig. Based on experiments with paranormal phenomena such as out-of-the-body experiences and telekinesis, the Mind Extractor used the cryogenic process to engender a near-death sense in the occupant's body, so that consciousness would ready itself for departure. Using a highly ingenious VR rig, the consciousness would then be captured, or 'harvested' in Vegas Vacations terminology. This was fascinatingly esoteric paranormal science, but the only way to find out if it worked or not was by using live human subjects. This the League had been doing with wild abandon. Hundreds of people had randomly disappeared to fuel the hunger for experimental subjects. Those who had survived harvesting, instead of being released to roam free as intelligent data, were being kept in a small private databank in Barbados, undergoing further tests.

The League experiments had been taking place in a number of locations around the world. One of the Mind Extractors was in New York, another was in London, another in Tokyo, and most recently one had been shipped to Kuala Lumpur in Malaysia. The Malaysian model was a new and improved version, which was expected to be capable of a much higher harvesting success rate. Currently, out of every 100 test subjects on average only two would make it through the process alive – if you could call it that, as their bodies were always dispensed with. As well as a success rate more like 50 per cent, the new Malaysian Mind Extractor was also the first to be able to put consciousness back into bodies. Perhaps the Extropians had some new plans to swap minds and bodies, as Robert J White had done with rhesus monkey heads in the 20th century. What was curious, however, was that it was a different group of League of

Future Life members who had obtained the Malaysian booth. Only a few of them were in common with the main set of names that kept appearing in the experimental records. The most frequent was Albert Kolinsky, which intuition told me was probably the Albert I called No Nose. He was a Chief Futurologist with the League – one of the head honchos. He was also one of the founders of the Church of Zero, an ordained Bishop of the Abyss. It crossed my mind that Kolinsky was behind the majority of my unfortunate circumstances.

I was also wondering if Michelle had been captured as a test subject herself. According to Harry, if this was the case she hadn't been through the Mind Extraction process just yet because he was still tracking her body moving around New York. I hadn't managed to draw a direct link between the League of Future Life's activities with the Mind Extractors and the Pure Light Abacus. However, it was clear that cracking the various problems with the harvesting technique required the most potent processing power around, which the Abacus represented. The Abacus would be a pretty useful tool for Mind Extraction experiments.

It seemed like a fair guess that if the League had stolen the Abacus, it would be at one of the sites where Mind Extractors had been located. These were also predominately very close to Vegas Vacations salons implicated in mind invasion incidents. There had to be a link here too, presumably something along the lines of the Extropians wanting to populate their new digital frontier with the greatest brains around.

I was starting to get a very smug feeling that I was on top of things again. My next move was quite clear – investigate the Kuala Lumpur Mind Extractor. But first I felt a return to New York was in order. I was still concerned about Michelle, and felt I had to make some attempt to wrest her back from the League. My uncharacteristic streak of humanity was afflicting me once more.

Data snooping over, I shut down the Assist Portamate and handed it back to Darryl. He locked it away in his briefcase and we set off out of the machine room. Without a word, we traipsed back to the elevator, our only sound the raucous scrunching of my paper suit. I tried walking more carefully while we entered the elevator, but it didn't have much effect.

As the doors opened on the ground floor, we were met by two gun barrels.

"Step out of the elevator with your hands in the air!" barked one of the guards. Harry put on the biggest grin I'd ever seen and strolled out into the lobby with his open palms high above his head.

"Gentleman, we've been having a late night sabbatical. Didn't the fellow on the desk tell you?" inquired Harry, sounding more congenial than Santa Claus.

"There's no booths in the basement," countered the guard. "We heard rustlin' in the machine room corridor. You guys bin snooping for Hawaiian Holidays?" Hawaiian Holidays was Vegas Vacations' main competitor, but didn't have the same level of technical advancement or commercial success. "You guys are Hawaiians, right?" he continued. By now our entire group was out of the elevator, arms outstretched. Thun was circling round shiftily to the left. The silent guard nervously jerked his gun towards him, but it was too late. Thun spat at him and something went thwack on his forehead. The guard collapsed instantly, eyes staring lifelessly. His loquacious companion swung his weapon in Thun's direction and let off a couple of shots. Thun had already dived forward into a roll, so the bullets simply flashed past where he had been a split second earlier. Before the guard could target him properly, Thun was on his feet again right beside him. He'd dropped the bolt cutters before executing his roll, so was barehanded. He grabbed the guard's gun arm at the wrist and backfisted him in the face. The guard's nose collapsed into a bloody mess. Then Thun gripped the man's face with his entire hand, ensuring the gun arm was still pointing away from anyone's direction. As the guard let off a couple more forlorn shots, Thun snapped the man's head back, fracturing his neck and nearly pulling the cranium clean off. Then he let the dead guard slump to the floor. It all happened in a matter of seconds, and not long afterwards Darryl had disposed of the evidence with his Nanotech aerosol. It was time for a swift exit.

* * *

As we drove away from Vegas Vacations, sirens wailed throughout the building we'd left behind. I made sure I had Thun in view from the corner of my eye - not that it would have done me any good. If he wanted me dead, Thun would have performed the deed in the time it took for someone's car horn to sound after traffic lights go green.

"Sorry about the rustling, Harry," I apologised. "That was why I wanted to get changed before we came." Harry flashed his characteristically broad grin.

"Not a problem!" he said, flapping his hand as if to brush away my apologetic tone. "Perhaps now you see why I am always smiling. With a man like Thun as my bodyguard, I have a reason to be relaxed. He is a genetically enhanced killing machine. He never fails."

Freida wasn't in when I got back to my room at the Caligula. I had no idea where she was. She hadn't been very happy when I'd headed off to The Senate bar on the night of our wedding. The surgically upholstered bimbo was probably relieving her annoyance by seducing some hapless visitor to Las Vegas. It wasn't a major problem whether she came back or not. She would only have gotten in the way anyhow. The plan I'd made with Harry was to get some rest that evening, then make an early start to New York, followed by a trip to Malaysia. I undressed and relaxed on the huge four-poster divan which anachronistically dominated the centre of this Roman-themed suite. I turned on the large viewing screen opposite the bed. It was set to the news channel, currently discussing the Scottish peace process. After a quick global weather bulletin came the local news.

"Las Vegas police were puzzled when they answered a call-out to Vegas Vacations head office on the strip tonight. Gunshots had been detected, but there were no obvious signs of a break-in past the main gate. Hand gun rounds found lodged in the lobby roof were the only evidence that there'd been a disturbance. Surveillance records showed no signs of any intruders, apart from some curious rustling sounds that were recorded moving around the building. Nothing had been stolen from the premises. In fact the only things missing were three security guards. A fourth guard who slept through the whole incident has been taken into custody for questioning."

This kept me smiling through more mundane subsequent stories about traffic problems and the exploits of a famous Vegas lap dancer who'd founded a successful teledildonics empire. Then I noticed a little camera symbol starting to flash in the top right hand corner of the screen. It was an incoming video message. I accepted the call and was almost pleasantly surprised to see Vanessa Carmichael's stern face filling the screen, larger than life.

"Oh, Dean, really," she began. It took me a few seconds to realise that I was still naked and probably visible in all my glory. The situation reminded me of why video telephones were still not universal. The last thing you wanted was to accept a call from your wife while in mid-coitus with your mistress. It could rather contradict your story about working late on an important new contract.

"Sorry, Vanessa," I replied, quickly covering myself with a bed sheet. "I wasn't really expecting you to call."

"I can imagine you weren't. We thought you were dead for a while, after the mix-up at your flat. Then we learnt from some friends that you were in Vegas. Having a little flutter? Feeling lucky, are you?"

"Lucky isn't really the word that springs to mind for me right now, Vanessa," I confided. "So what exactly happened to my flat?

Those were COSI operatives, weren't they?"

"Yes, with the emphasis on the past tense in some cases, Bentley." The statement felt like a scolding from my mother.

"Well, it's a dog eat dog world, Vanessa," I replied defensively. "I know you'd have done the same."

"Maybe not quite with your death toll, Bentley, but I suppose so. They were told that The Newt was hiding out at your address. He's wanted for the bombing of the McDonalds headquarters. The entire Pacify or Terminate squad was mobilised. We're still trying to work out where the wrong information came from. It was logged in all of our automatic callout systems, with all the right authorisation from me. Except I never authorised it. Anyway, how have you been doing?"

I couldn't be bothered to lie to Carmichael, so I explained everything. I even mentioned my joining forces with the Thai Free State. Carmichael's hint of a smile told me she already knew about that. I left out the parts about Michelle, though. Something made me want to keep that bit secret. I thought it would make me look weak.

"I'm sorry I couldn't attend your wedding," remarked Carmichael, wryly. "Congratulations, though. I never thought you had it in you to make an honest woman out of anyone!" I almost laughed out loud at the idea of anyone making Freida into an honest woman. The very concept was a paradox. Carmichael informed me that my mission had expanded to include finding the Pure Light Abacus and returning it to its owners. Apparently, the reward from the Mao laboratory's parent company was going to be extensive, from which I would of course receive a bonus. She congratulated me on my work so far, saying it was way beyond what she'd expected of me.

Before the praise got too awkward, the hotel room door swung open with a crash and Freida barged in drunkenly. Her very short skirt wasn't on straight, and her blouse wasn't buttoned properly either. She turned jerkily towards the screen and waved a hand sloppily at Carmichael.

"So you prefer spending a night watching this old biddy on screen to having some fun with me? I want a divorce!"

Eyeing Freida tiredly, I introduced her to Carmichael, explaining that Vanessa was my godmother, and that I'd wanted to tell her the glorious news of my getting hitched. Freida pouted, but seemed to believe me, too drunk to raise the question of what kind of godmother you talk to naked in bed. I then bade Vanessa farewell and terminated the video link. Freida stumbled towards the bathroom, where she was violently sick. After she'd finished, there were a few bangs and crashes accompanied by a range of clumsy expletives, then the sound of running water. Part of me felt like checking if she was okay; but mostly I was hoping she would run a bath and then drown in it. I returned to watching the viewing screen.

Just as I was beginning to get drowsy, I heard the bathroom door open. Through my half-closed eyes, I could just make out Freida's silhouette. She was wearing see-through lingerie so small it would have looked skimpy on a Barbie doll. She posed in the doorway in a drunken parody of seduction, then attempted to catwalk to the bed. Instead, she failed to notice my shoes on the floor and fell forward, banging her head on the side of the bed. Freida was a resilient girl, though, and without any shame. Instead of falling unconscious, she simply continued toward the bed on all fours, dragged herself onto it, and began to make her needs plain. Reluctantly, I acquiesced.

Log 000111011111 – Gambling and putting your trust in God are part of the same subconscious realisation that you are not really in control of your destiny. However far the power of technology over life goes, there's always an element of chance. Either you believe a supreme being dictates the quality of your luck, or you believe nothing does at all.

Freida was still fast asleep when I left the hotel room. She looked contented. I knew I'd see her again – she'd pursue me like a dog after a flying stick, and with just as little reason. But it was time to move on without surplus baggage. I met Harry and his gang in the lobby and we headed for the Microsoft Hotel for breakfast. We ended up in the Windows Bar and Grill – an impressive all-glass restaurant atop the tallest tower in Vegas. Unfortunately, they got my order wrong twice, but the third time they delivered something closer to what I wanted. Successive courses got slightly better each time.

I had to leave the Skycar in Vegas. Harry had a brand new Learjet on call, and that was an infinitely more comfortable way to travel to New York, and much quicker. If I needed individual transportation again I could always steal something. The Learjet was a supersonic magnetic E3500, capable of just under 1,500 miles per hour and built for luxury. The journey took scarcely three hours, but it felt like less thanks to the freely flowing champagne and high class snacks. We arrived in New York in time for lunch, which Harry had booked at a Southeast Asian restaurant called Ipoh on the East Side. We dropped our things off at his penthouse on 50th and 2nd Avenue. It was at the top of a cigar-shaped tower called The Clinton, a 180-floor behemoth with great balcony views across 50th Street and down 2nd Avenue. If ever I'd felt like retiring, this would have been my kind of hideaway.

After a spicy meal of soft shell crabs at Ipoh, we drove in Harry's black Mercedes to the far western side of the West Village, into what used to be the meat-packing district in the early 20th century.

We stopped on Gansevoort St at a building which had originally been built as a frozen chicken warehouse over a hundred years ago. More recently it had been the delivery address of one of the specially-converted Mind Extractor cryogenic sabbatical booths. The building turned out to be the Central Tabernacle of the Church of Zero – Zeroastrianism's equivalent of the Vatican. Harry, Thun and I left Darryl in the car and entered. During our journey from Las Vegas, Harry had made further enquiries and ascertained that this was also the last location recorded for Michelle's homing beacon. Perhaps here was the place where I would be able to tie up two mysteries in one.

A service was taking place in the Tabernacle. A group of fashionably-attired code jockeys taking a break from their Silicon Alley programming jobs were getting their spiritual sustenance. At the front of the group, a bald, pale and dangerously thin high priest stood dressed in a horribly clashing array of fluorescently-coloured clothing. He was leading the intoning of the prayer:

"Our father, who art in nothingness,
Hollow be thy name.
Your kingdom's done,
Your will is none…"

And so it continued. We waited at the back of the Tabernacle hall until the congregation had finished its prayers and trooped up to the priest to receive a pill. Known as Mellow, this was a drug of questionable legality loosely based around the outlawed Prozac. It was supposed to cure Zeroastrians of placing too much value on any material item or emotional state. With the help of Mellow, disciples of the Church of Zero believed they would remain liberated from the constraints of the illusory material world, and become free to act. It regularly amused me how groups of people adopted a universal style or religion in the belief that it would make them free individuals. The only way to make yourself an individual was to be one. These Zeroastrians, despite their highly sophisticated rebellion from all pre-existing universal rules and mores, had simply succeeded in creating a new set of morals to follow. In their striving to be different, they just ended up acting the same. They even dressed alike, with their studiedly-sloppy casual wear and deliberate denial of personal hygiene. I wondered how long it would be before some of them realised they were all virtually identical, and broke free to form yet another sect so the whole process could start all over again.

After the programmers had left the Tabernacle, we approached the high priest, who was paying us little attention while he packed away the few symbolic items used in the ceremony. It was surprising that he should be left alone in such an important place for Zeroastrianism, but perhaps that was indicative of their beliefs. The priest was concentrating intently on placing a black sphere, a large child-proof bottle containing Mellow, and a phallic sceptre into a specially-compartmentalised aluminium flight case. When we got a few feet away, however, he turned towards us with a big smile. He held his palms open and facing upwards in the kind of pose often used to depict Jesus in earlier centuries.

"Brothers! How can I help you?" the priest enquired. "In need of release from the heavy weight of social convention? You must free your mind from the masses! The time is now!"

"Er, no, Reverend," I replied. "We're looking for a girl. About five and half feet tall, reddish hair, called Michelle."

It was very fortunate that the priest hadn't chosen a career in acting. His attempt at denying all knowledge of any girl with a shrug and a grimace was about as convincing as a Jehovah's Witness. He was easily betrayed by the fraught look in his eyes as he kept glancing at Thun. Feeling upstaged by the huge Thai, I pulled out my pistol and shoved it up the priest's left nostril.

"Where is she?" I shouted. Again the priest shrugged, but this time he appeared to be telling the truth.

"I, I, I," he stammered, "d...d...d...don't n...n...know." It's amazing how the prospect of a premature death can turn even the most ardent nihilist into a gibbering wreck. I grabbed the priest by his shirt and dragged him through the door at the back of the hall. Harry and his entourage followed. Pinning the unresisting Reverend down onto a table in the back room, I pistol whipped him a little around the face until his nose was bloody. It wasn't really necessary. The pathetic guy was already offering to tell us everything, including many things we didn't actually want to know. But a small amount of violence just for effect always makes an interrogation more poetic, or at any rate more enjoyable.

Apparently, Michelle had been held at the Tabernacle for the last few days, but had been taken away a couple of hours before our arrival. The Tabernacle was regularly used by the League of Future Life as a safe house. The way the Church of Zero helped the League out, it was almost as if the Zeroastrians were the religious wing of the League. Their two philosophies matched so well, as if they were destined to be together – the Church providing the religious underpinnings for what the League put into practice. However, the League was an illegal underground organisation, whereas the Church of Zero was a legitimate registered religion. It could even perform marriages, as I'd discovered to my cost in Las Vegas. I stood over the high priest, gun in hand, my incredulity growing as he spouted Zeroastrian doctrine at me ever more frantically, and divulged the locations of hoards of valuable equipment. Like the League, the Church made a cult out of the idea of transcendence through technology. Mankind's destiny and will was to leave the constraints of the individual body and join together into one consciousness. Ever more powerful computing was to be the vehicle by which the human will would become free of the physical world. It didn't take a great leap of imagination to guess how the Pure Light Abacus would fit into all this.

Behind me I heard Harry talking into his phone. He'd left Santada back at the apartment researching and keeping an eye out for any more reports on Michelle's whereabouts. She'd obviously found something useful. I returned my attention to the high priest and asked him where he kept his cryogenic sabbatical booth. Sheepishly, he led me downstairs. Harry and Thun brought up the rear. The booth didn't look any different to the ones I'd seen in Vegas, except that it had a large rack of computer equipment next to it. The priest explained that this was required to control the mind extraction process. The rack had vast amounts of local storage in which to keep a freshly-harvested consciousness before it was emailed as an attachment to the League's central storage facility in Barbados. Occasionally, the mail would go missing and the consciousness would have to be resent. I had a very quick run through the console, but realised it would take days to figure out how everything worked. Instead, I ordered the high priest into the booth, turned the setting up to medium and the timer on for a week, and left him.

I'd never liked religions of any sort, especially since my father died in a bizarre trepanning accident when I was still very young. At least, that's what the other members of the Wicca sect he'd been a member of claimed in court. They got away with it, but I wasn't so sure of their innocence. It's not so easy to bore a hole in your own skull with a hand drill. My theory was that they'd found out he was researching for a TV show on violence amongst the English druidic population and they'd decided to shut him up. This was before the running battles between new age travellers and police had led to a nationwide ban on druids and earth religions. My dad's sect was one of the worst culprits, and was eventually found to be practicing child sacrifice. When I was old enough, I tracked down each of the Wiccan druids in turn and exacted my own revenge with a masonry chisel as a trepanning device. I'd figured a hand drill was too good for them. I was a very angry young man in those days, but already a pro at covering my tracks. Even though I was a prime suspect, there was no evidence to pin the killings on me, so I got away with them. That was really how my life on the shadier side began. I was deprived of my Oedipus complex, because somebody else had already killed my father.

Harry explained that Santada had fresh information about Michelle's current destination. Local tracking equipment had pinpointed her a few hours previously at JFK airport. She'd boarded a private jet which was now heading West across the country. Harry suggested dinner at his favourite Eritrean restaurant before we set off in pursuit in his Learjet. The other aircraft had a major head start, but now we were tracking it via a hack into US air traffic control, so keeping tabs on its location was easy. From Santada's calculations, Harry's Learjet had a much faster cruising speed than the League's aircraft. We would quickly catch up with the other plane before it left US air space. Still, I was sad not to get a single night in Harry's penthouse, although I'd noticed Harry's Learjet had seats that converted into proper beds. At least I was going to get a comfortable place to sleep.

The Eritrean food was superb, and Harry was on top form. As we all tucked into a variety of spicy dishes including minced raw beef, he reeled off story upon story about his childhood running a ping-pong show in Bangkok. That was before he moved on to what he called pharmaceutical trading and became one of the most influential men in Thailand. It was late evening by the time we boarded the Learjet. I didn't feel like sleeping, but the conversation had calmed down considerably since dinner. So I found a plush seat near the back of the craft and settled in to absorb some mindless entertainment on the viewing screen. After a bit of surfing, I found a live feed called "Grafted". At the beginning of each week of the series, two people with diametrically opposed opinions on the world were surgically attached to each-other and sent on a variety of dates, with potentially hilarious consequences. This week, a transsexual had been bonded onto an Islamic fundamentalist. It was an interactive show during which viewers could choose the day's activities – for example, whether the Grafted contestants would go to a mosque or head off for a night out in a fetish nightclub. At the end of the week, assuming the contestants hadn't killed each-other, the audience voted on whether or not the pair would be offered the opportunity to be separated and have any shared organs replaced. If they were separated, they also received a generous prize cheque. It was all pretty standard stuff. What particularly interested me in the show was that it was sponsored by the Monsignor medical company. The telltale panda logo was everywhere, from the chevron in the top left corner to the branding of any hats and tee-shirts worn by the participants.

Grafted passed the time for an hour or so, then I had a couple of drinks and took a nap. I was woken by a stewardess who informed me that we'd soon be landing. Harry's snooping had tracked the League jet to Los Angeles, where it had touched down about twenty minutes previously. Santada's more personal tracking told us that Michelle hadn't left the plane. A few further inquiries with the LA ground staff ascertained that the other jet was merely refuelling for the next hop. Darryl organised the same for the Learjet. About an hour later they took off again, and fifteen minutes after that so did we. For the next three hours we continued to follow the League jet, keeping out of visual range at high altitude. As well as being faster, our aircraft could fly much greater distances between refuelling stops than our quarry, so we could afford to go wherever it went without fear of running out of juice. Once we were in Asia, too, we'd have access to Harry's extensive local spy network. This would make it simple to keep tabs on the jet and its occupants without having to follow so closely.

Whilst I slept some more, our route took us past Japan and over the Philippines. Judging from my research at Vegas Vacations, it was a safe bet that we were heading for Malaysia, where the League had shipped its most sophisticated Mind Extractor. I'd estimated the time of arrival in Kuala Lumpur at our current speed and set my alarm for half an hour beforehand, so I could grab a quick snack before we landed. My hunch as to our destination was unsurprisingly correct, although my timing was about ten minutes too late. I rubbed the sleep from my eyes whilst Harry jovially informed me how both the League and our aircraft had been intercepted by a couple of Chinese fighters. As paranoid as China was, this kind of behaviour seemed rather unusual in international airspace, particular as our own vehicles were relatively innocuous civilian models. The Chinese pilots had asked a few questions about destinations and purposes, then screamed off elsewhere.

As the League jet made its final approach to Kuala Lumpur, I wolfed down a portion of the cranberry salad we'd stocked up with in LA and plied myself with coffee to revive my attention after the power naps. Twenty minutes passed and then our Learjet was taxiing down the tarmac at New KLIA airport. It was late evening, around the same time locally as we'd left New York, but in Malaysia it was pitch black outside the window apart from the runway lights. New York had been shrouded by a pleasant grey dusk during our takeoff, but the Malaysian darkness was deceptive. Even though it was well into night time, I knew the outside temperature would still be pushing thirty degrees centigrade. At least in Malaysia's oppressively hot climate my rustling paper suit could have a genuine practical use, that was if we ever happened to be caught out of air-conditioned space.

Log 000111110001 – The best way to achieve a perfect hard-boiled egg is to cook it for longer at a lower temperature. The problem with using a higher temperature is that the white gets overcooked before the yoke is fully hard. Cooking at a lower heat means the cooking is more evenly distributed, so the yoke is properly cooked but the white is not overdone.

The old Kuala Lumpur International Airport had been torn down a decade previously. For a few weeks in the late Twentieth Century it had been the largest open space in the world, until Hong Kong's new air facility on a reclaimed island stole the Malaysians' thunder. Just before the old International Airport in Malaysia met its demise, though, the little South East Asian tiger had taken back some pride by building the tallest airport outside of China. New Kuala Lumpur International Airport, or NKLIA as the locals liked to call it, had eaten up a massive expanse of the jungle, even though it was multi-level. Once they'd landed, aircraft taxied to slots stacked on top of each-other, reducing the time it took for passengers to move from their planes to connecting flights or external transportation. With supersonic jets becoming more the norm than the exception, it had become increasingly important to reduce passengers' airport time as well as their flight time. NKLIA was very good at this, apart from during the first few days after opening, when computer systems chaos meant that 300 people went missing. Twenty-five of them still were. Myths abounded that these score and five continued to wander the fifteen vaulted floors of NKLIA, unable to find their way out of the maze of check-in desks and concessionary stands. Malaysian mothers made their children behave by telling them horror stories about the fate of these Lost Ones, although the authorities really wanted to forget the incident ever happened.

Harry's jet was directed towards a slot on one of the private levels of NKLIA. We taxied into the loading lift, where the aircraft was raised to the fifth floor. An automatic tractor system hauled us to our disembarkation slot. Within ten minutes of landing we were gathering our belongings together and heading for the cabin door. I felt fine, although with the constant travel my body now had no idea what time it was. At least I'd slept and eaten something. NKLIA had all the latest automatic customs and immigration systems, so we were able to walk straight off the plane towards ground transportation. Harry had already contacted his local operation and a massive BMW limousine was waiting for us in the car park. The Malaysian chauffeur met us at the gate, waving excitedly a paper sign which read "Harry Sivaraksa".

"Mr Sivaraksa, sir. We welcome you to visit our humble business. This operation very profitable-lah."

The chauffeur then pointed out that he was more than just a humble driver. Harry's local management figured that Harry deserved someone who could show him around the city and various offices. His name was N D Wong and he was an associate manager with Sivtronix, one of Harry's legal front companies. Sivtronix specialised in telecommunications and wireless devices. Wong was an ethnic Chinese Malaysian, as indeed were many of Harry's staff in Malaysia. Harry had set the company up in the fabled Malaysian Multimedia Super Corridor, so the requirement of a Malay business partner had been waived.

Despite the size of the BMW, there were only just enough seats for all of us. Thun rode up front with Wong, who rather irritatingly insisted on providing a few choice facts about every sizeable office building we passed. Wong must have thought he was giving an industrialist's sightseeing tour. I dreaded to think what he had lined up for the evening's entertainment – probably a virtual karaoke session. In between interruptions, Harry discussed our plan of action with us. First we were going to drop off our luggage at his penthouse in Bangsar, a district of Kuala Lumpur known for its expatriate community. Then we'd grab a quick noodle soup supper cum early breakfast at a hawker shop, before heading off to wherever the League had taken Michelle. This was something I particularly liked about Harry - he was never in too much of a hurry to eat.

Harry's Bangsar apartment topped even his New York residence, and had me wondering what I'd been doing wrong all these years. Situated on the top floor of a 153-storey block, it boasted a roof palm tree orchard, a fully air-conditioned conservatory housing a massive Jacuzzi, and seven bedrooms. Something told me, however, that here again I would not get a chance to enjoy the luxury before we moved on. Indeed, we were scarcely in the apartment for ten minutes before heading back to the elevator. Wong drove us the few short blocks to what he explained was the most famous hawker shop in Bangsar. Apparently, it had the best Ngau Lam broth in Kuala Lumpur. I was looking forward to trying this special soup until I discovered it consisted of all the bits of a cow you don't usually eat stewed up together for hours. You never knew what you'd be getting until you tucked in to eat, and frankly I wasn't going to give myself an opportunity to find out. I chose a simple plate of chicken rice instead.

After our meal in the only just bearably air-conditioned shop, the BMW slid up to the pavement outside. We braved the sweltering heat of the street for the few brief seconds it took to climb inside the limo's refrigerated interior. This was modern day life in the tropics – you scarcely noticed the temperature because everywhere you went was climate-controlled. In fact, I even felt a little cold in the BMW. Again, Thun sat up front while the rest of us enjoyed the plush leather-upholstered rear. Harry pulled a decanter of cognac from the small bar in the middle of the passenger area and poured a few glasses. I managed to stop him just before he added water and ice to mine. It was clearly good French cognac, and would have been expensive in this predominately Muslim country. Watering it down was not the way to do it justice. It would also have reduced the warming capability I craved in the icy air conditioning.

Our conversation was sparse as we travelled south through the city towards the Multimedia Super Corridor. Not surprisingly, this was where Santada had tracked Michelle's beacon. We were headed towards a lab owned by StrongMan Armaments, another firm like Monsignor involved in exploiting discoveries in human genomics. StrongMan, however, was in the defence rather than medical industry. After an hour on the smooth, well-surfaced Kuala Lumpur highways, we joined the approach road to the Multimedia Super Corridor itself. Wong explained that were it light, we'd see the leafy garden city of Putrajaya on our left. Proudly, he promised to show us the beautiful new city on our return – for it was where he lived. The road circled around Putrajaya, and headed towards CJ, which was what the locals called another garden city by the name of Cyberjaya. CJ was the main organisational centre of the Multimedia Super Corridor where the government administration was situated. We had to go through it to reach the industrial estates and science parks of the Corridor proper.

Wong seemed crestfallen as Harry directed him past the Sivtronix buildings. He had clearly been looking forward for most of his adult life, and probably his childhood as well, to showing Chairman Sivaraksa around his company's Malaysian operation. Instead, Harry explained, we were going to postpone the tour until the following day. First we had important business with StrongMan Armaments. The StrongMan building was short and squat compared to the majority of Corridor companies' gleaming towers. Santada's intelligence report told us that StrongMan was still a tall building, but that most of its length went underground rather than upwards. I wasn't sure what Harry's plan was, but I didn't fancy the chances of a similar full-frontal attack to the one we'd performed in Vegas. Two very serious-looking automatic gun posts guarded the main gate as we pulled up. Even Thun wouldn't have been immune to the 20mm-calibre weaponry very obviously emplaced in each.

Fortunately, Harry wasn't considering any kind of breaking and entering this time. As a respected chairman of a neighbouring high tech company, he'd booked an early meeting with a top StrongMan executive. The magic words "merger talks" had been all it had taken to attract StrongMan's attention, especially as it came from an electronics company with some very advanced surveillance technologies, an ideal marriage to StrongMan's weaponry business. The time was about five o'clock in the morning, and the meeting was for five thirty. Our BMW was permitted through the gates without mishap, and we purred through the dark towards the lobby of the main office. I felt very nervous as we entered. Although the League had no reason to suspect Harry, if there were any of them about who recognised me our cover would be blown immediately. This didn't seem to worry Harry unduly, but I dreaded to think what kinds of torture a company like StrongMan could conjure up for Albert Kolinsky to deploy upon my body. My brief stint cooking in the cryogenic sabbatical booth had been bad enough, and this time I doubted Freida would be waiting around the corner to save me. At least we had Thun, our secret weapon.

A massive, square-jawed security guard led us to a spacious meeting room and bade us sit down. The conference table was made out of a single, shiny block of dark wood astride thick brushed-aluminium legs. The green leather swivel chairs arranged neatly around it were plush and comfortable. I couldn't keep from nervously swivelling mine from side to side as we waited. We were rather early, so it was twenty minutes before the meeting room doors swung open again and the StrongMan representatives entered.

My heart immediately sank. Heading the StrongMan group was exactly the person I didn't want to see: Albert Kolinsky. He smiled straight at me and took his place at the head of the conference table. He was accompanied by six more chisel-faced security guards. With a jolt I realised they were all identical twins. The guards were either an advanced form of robot or clones. Either way, they were all heavily armed and huge. Thun would be able to take a few of them out in succession, but not six at the same time. We weren't going anywhere.

"Good to see you again, Dean," chuckled Kolinsky, clearly very pleased with himself. "I was expecting you. But I'll deal with you in a minute." He turned his attention to Harry. "Now, about that merger. I presume you'll be handing control of Sivtronix to StrongMan?"

Harry wasn't looking quite as happy as normal, but he hadn't lost his cool. With a beaming smile, he brushed aside Kolinsky's demand.

"Albert, that sounds more like a hostile takeover! You're getting your business terms mixed up! But we do have some common interests, which I think are represented very nicely by our mutual friend Mr Dean here." Harry motioned towards me. "There are ways we could be mutually beneficial. Darryl, show Mr Kolinsky the merger documents."

Darryl, who'd been sitting calmly with his brief-case on the desk in front of him, popped the catches. Before he could open the case, though, he was dead. One of the angular clone guards had drawn a handgun with lightning reflexes and shot Darryl precisely in the middle of the forehead. His brain was liberally spattered all over the wall behind him as the rear half of his skull shattered. He jolted lifelessly back in his chair and then slumped forward. Now Harry was looking angry. He crossed his hands in front of him on the table. Santada had a tear rolling down her cheek. It was fortunate Mr Wong was still with the car, or he'd have been hysterical. Thun was the only one to remain impassive. He was leaning comfortably back in his arm chair, as he had been since we entered the room.

"Maybe a hostile takeover was more what I had in mind, Mr Sivaraksa," continued Kolinsky, who was wearing a different-shaped nose from the one I'd seen him in at Vegas Vacations. Harry shook his head tiredly.

"This is just not the way to do business in Asia, Mr Kolinsky. You have no understanding of the etiquette we use here. It was very rude of you to terminate one of my best employees for attempting to open his briefcase." Harry's right forefinger, which had slowly snaked its way towards his watch as he clasped his hands together, pressed a button on the timepiece and there was an audible click. "Especially when I am the one with the trigger to the explosive devices inside." Harry's smile returned, although this time it looked very forced. "The trigger is linked to my vital signs, so you can be assured if you kill me or render me unconscious, Mr Kolinsky, most of this building will be demolished, and you with it."

It was Albert's turn to lose his smile. Before he could reply, Harry continued:

"I would like your clone army to leave the room. Then we can get down to business. The one who shot my associate shall remain, unarmed." Harry sat back with his arms crossed for a few seconds. "I'm waiting."

"And if I don't you'll kill us all?" enquired Albert with a sneer that betrayed a hint of nervousness. He was not entirely convinced by Harry's ultimatum.

"Mr Kolinsky, you should know I have the technology, but you question my will. That is not a very sensible position, considering the intelligence you must have about the way I do business." Harry must have had a reputation for ruthlessness I hadn't yet discovered, as Kolinsky looked at his feet momentarily, then ordered five of the six guards to leave. They didn't have names – just numbers. The remaining guard, who'd relinquished his sidearm to one of his fellows, was called 73. As soon as the doors were shut, Harry reached across to Darryl's briefcase and retrieved strange-looking handgun. After adjusting a setting, he shot the guard, who slumped to his knees and began foaming at the mouth. "A nasty poison. Hours of pain and no known antidote. Would you like to give it a try, Mr Kolinsky?" Harry nodded to Thun, who rose from his seat and approached Kolinsky. "Hurt him a little first, Thun," commanded Harry.

Thun rabbit-punched Kolinsky squarely in the face, squashing his prosthetic nose inwards. It remained perched there, flattened ridiculously, as Thun grabbed one of Kolinsky's hands and effortlessly snapped a couple of the fingers backwards. No Nose, or more appropriately Flat Nose at that particular moment, whimpered a little and blanched white.

"So," resumed Harry. "The deal I had in mind was rather different to yours. I would like to know the whereabouts of the Pure Light Abacus, which I am confident would make an acceptable recompense for the loss of my valuable employee here."

"Fuck," replied Albert, who obviously had a low tolerance for pain. "Can't tell you..." Harry nodded towards Thun, who broke a few more fingers. "It's – not – here!" He gurgled. Then Albert Kolinsky lost consciousness, falling towards Thun, who nonchalantly let him rebound off his ample pectorals and plummet to the floor. Harry asked Santada to revive Kolinsky. When the injured man was awake again, Harry asked for a tour of the StrongMan facility. Kolinsky reluctantly acquiesced, a resigned look on his now nose-less face. Half of me was full of glee that No Nose was getting some retribution. In fact, so was the other half. I was a very happy man.

Thun took Harry's poison gun from him and jammed it into No Nose's back. Harry gestured that we should all rise from our seats. We left the meeting room and headed for an elevator. The clone guards were outside but made no attempt to rescue their boss as he took us down to the penultimate floor of the underground facility. Harry had particularly requested to see the cryogenic sabbatical booth. En route, we got a glimpse of some of StrongMan's sophisticated weapons systems in their test labs. The 20mm SM2020 handheld recoilless caught my particular attention. It looked like a pistol for shooting flares, but was far less innocent. Its ammo could penetrate thick walls, all forms of body armour, and would pretty much kill any living creature from a blue whale downwards with one shot. Lasers had come a long way, but you still couldn't beat a decent projectile weapon in my opinion. With the SM2020 in your pocket you could face a small armoured vehicle with confidence. I picked up a prototype from a lab table plus a pack of ammo and stuffed it inside my jacket.

The genetics labs were even more sinister. Robotic and human body parts were strewn side by side on lab benches and it was hard to tell the difference between them. A human head and torso, exactly like one of the clone guards, was lying naked on an operating table. I couldn't make out whether it was alive or dead. As it was still very early in the morning, there were only one or two technicians working in the lab, and they didn't pay us much attention. This was despite the fact that No Nose, who'd recovered considerably from the initial shock of his finger injuries, was starting to go into considerable detail about what StrongMan was developing. Clearly, Malaysia made everyone want to be a proud tour guide. According to Kolinsky, the guards we came across earlier were a prototype StrongMan product branded Syborgs. They were a complicated amalgam of cloning techniques and grafting. Refined genetic code was used to grow body parts with the ultimate in physical characteristics. These were then grafted together into whole bodies. Robotic parts could be mixed and matched, depending on the use intended for the final product. You could even embed weaponry like the SM2020 or advanced machine tools. Mentally, however, the clone assemblies were not that advanced. Accelerated human brain development was still in its infancy, and these humanoids could only be kept alive for a year or so apiece before the immune responses to the many transplants, or the drugs used to counteract them, caused complete physical collapse. With such a short time to learn about the world, even with genetically enhanced mental powers, the Syborgs could only be taught to excel at physical tasks. Their thought processes were childish and primitive.

As we'd already discovered at Vegas Vacations, the League had been experimenting with technology to extract the consciousness from one cerebral cortex and download it into another. But the Syborgs' clone brains were not receptive to the process. Their synaptic pathways were too underdeveloped to accept the quantity of information in a mature human consciousness. This was a major drawback. The long-term goal of StrongMan, a company wholly owned by Extropian League members, was to provide a complete package. They wanted their customers to be able to transfer themselves to a modular, upgradeable Syborg body. But they needed an alternative brain-cloning technique to realise their intentions.

Industrial espionage had come to the rescue. A spy at Monsignor discovered that the medical company had found a way of massively accelerating the maturation of foetal clones. Fully-developed humans could be grown in vats in a few years. Unlike StrongMan's assemblages of parts, the Monsignor clone had a naturally, if speedily developed brain. The League wanted this technology, so about two years previously they'd attempted to steal one of the prototypes from the Newcastle Monsignor facility. However, the Syborgs used in the mission had botched the job. The whole incident had miraculously been kept away from the media, but it had been a major mess. There had been carnage, with a number of clone specimens destroyed and important researchers killed. Worst of all, instead of being captured, the main prototype had escaped from the lab and disappeared. Fortunately, a stroke of luck had relocated her recently. I figured the beneficent fortune they were referring to was provided by me, although it all seemed too much of a coincidence. Michelle was the Monsignor prototype. By Kolinski's description, she was only five years old – three years in the vat, two on the streets. But her genetically engineered mind picked things up much more quickly than natural humans. She was physically and mentally in her late teens. Monsignor had developed Michelle for testing new drugs, and the League and StrongMan had even worse plans for her. The thought of someone being grown just so someone else could take over their body seemed pretty repulsive, and I'd led this scumbag right to her. I almost pulled out the SM2020 and gave No Nose a new, extra large nasal cavity right there, but I figured it wouldn't be polite as he was in mid-sentence.

Continuing his story, Kolinsky told us how things had not gone quite to plan over the last few hours, after they'd brought Michelle to the lab for a consciousness transplant. There seemed to have been a malfunction as they put her in the Mind Extractor. Instead of removing her consciousness, the Extractor had downloaded something to her brain, probably a virus. After that, she'd started behaving strangely, babbling something vaguely religious-sounding about cows and crocodiles. The Mind Extractor was currently undergoing major diagnostics to find out what had gone wrong. Michelle was locked in a cage on another floor, raving. StrongMan scientists hadn't yet started to analyse her to work out what damage had occurred, but No Nose feared Michelle's potential had been spoilt. He was despondent. He had wanted her to be reverse engineered so StrongMan could install cerebrums based around her cloning design into his company's Syborgs. Now it looked like they wouldn't be able to ensure the process would work beforehand. It could all have been a massive waste of time and money.

"So I guess she wasn't The One after all," I quipped. No Nose looked nonplussed.

"What do you mean?" he asked. I explained about the New York note, but he claimed not to know anything about it. I didn't really believe him. If the note wasn't from the League, it was a mystery who'd sent it. This was one coincidence too many – the note had arrived, and a few hours later Michelle was kidnapped by the League. They had to have been responsible. I asked No Nose to take us to Michelle. I wanted to make my own damage assessment, and then maybe it would be time to move Albert Kolinsky's membership from the League of Future Life to the Society of Recent Dead.

Log 000111110010 – One of the differences between a living organism and a machine is that living beings are unpredictable. If we ever come to understand the organic as well as well as we understand machines, perhaps we'd discover that organisms were just complicated mechanisms all along. Or maybe we'd realise that machines behaving unpredictably could be showing signs of life.

Michelle was sleeping curled up in one corner of her cage when we arrived. She looked quite peaceful until No Nose's incessant jabbering woke her. Then she leapt from her corner and flung her body at the bars like an angry ape, cursing Kolinsky and her imprisonment. After a series of insults that wouldn't have passed on TV even after the midnight watershed, she noticed me and Harry and her anger suddenly fell away.

"Hello, Bentley!" she exclaimed with strange enthusiasm. "You came for me. How sweet. And you're called Harry, aren't you? Where is that other nice boy? Darryl wasn't it?"

"I'm afraid he's no longer with us due to the lack of consideration of this fellow here," explained Harry, with a dismissive nod of his head towards Kolinsky. "Thun, release her from this monkey prison." With his usual efficiency and speed, Thun unhooked a multi-tool from his belt and chose a snipping implement. I wasn't convinced how something that could scarcely fit around the bars would make anything more than a scratch in the tough metal. The snipping implement must have been very sharp and strong, though, because in Thun's hands it sliced through the bars as if they were hollow cardboard tubes. In less than a minute Michelle was able to step out.

"Actually, I had the key," sulked No Nose. I looked at him accusingly for a second, then turned to Harry.

"Do we really need this guy anymore?" I protested. "Maybe we should get rid of him. I'll gladly offer my services if you like."

"I share your feelings, Bentley," replied Harry. "But we must keep our focus. We still have to find the Pure Light Abacus! That is the whole reason for our excursion here. I think Mr Kolinsky has important knowledge. The girl is incidental." Having said his piece, Harry looked around the laboratory, which was empty apart from us. "This seems like a good place, Thun. Ready the serum."

No Nose looked around worriedly, as if searching for an escape route, but this was futile with Thun training a deadly weapon on him. So instead he just stood there sheepishly while the Thai killing machine took a gas syringe out of Darryl's briefcase and jabbed him in the side of the neck. Kolinski's body twitched a bit, then Harry began asking him questions about the Pure Light Abacus. The drug ensured that he answered truthfully, and it was a lot more effective than the sodium pentathol of old.

Kolinski was full of information. The Abacus had not been stolen by the League of Future Life, and he didn't know who'd taken it. But he did know where it had been taken. The Abacus was in Israel, in New Tel Aviv. The League had managed to infiltrate the Mao Tse Tung facility in Andorra a few days before its destruction, but their own plan to obtain the Abacus hadn't reached fruition before someone else came along and grabbed it. The League's undercover operative had been killed during the theft, leaving them in the dark as to who'd pre-empted their own heist. But a transmitter placed in the computer's central housing had allowed its movements to be tracked as it was transported by land to the south coast of France, and then by sea to Israel. That was where it had stayed for the previous two days. Just that morning, the League had dispatched a squad of its Syborgs to Israel to retrieve the Abacus and bring it to Malaysia. The Syborgs were to be arriving in the holy land in a few hours time. Harry got Kolinski to log into a nearby console and call up a map of where the Abacus was believed to be in Tel Aviv. He copied this over to the Assist Portamate I had used in Las Vegas, which was still in the late Darryl's briefcase. Then he signalled that our visit to the offices of StrongMan Defence Technology had come to an end, and it was time to get back to the car.

The smooth elevator took a matter of seconds to raise us back up to ground level. There were more people milling around the building by then, as normal working hours had arrived. Many looked at us apprehensively as we made our way to the main door, because Thun was still training the gun on Kolinsky's back. The Syborg guards we passed eyed us warily, but made no action to prevent our passage. Once we'd passed through the main door, Harry turned to Albert and retrieved something from Darryl's briefcase of tricks. It was a thick bracelet with a tough metal exterior, a wirelessly operated lock and an array of enigmatic flashing lights around its circumference.

"A little insurance policy. This is the bomb. Remember, I can trigger it remotely at any time, and it's locked into my vital signs." Harry locked the bracelet around Kolinski's wrist. "Send anyone against me, and you'll become a very noisy Chinese New Year celebration." I felt sure it wouldn't take Kolinski long to get the bomb off his person, but it would buy us enough time to get out of the Super Corridor and on our way, presumably to Israel.

The BMW was waiting for us, and so was Wong, oblivious to all that had transpired in the StrongMan building. He was so excited that he would now be taking us to see his beloved Sivtronix premises, he didn't even notice Thun hide the poison gun in a jacket pocket, nor the blanched look of fear on Kolinsky's face as Harry made him put on the bracelet. Wong didn't even remark upon Kolinsky's lack of a nose, or the loss of Darryl to be replaced by Michelle. But it wasn't to be long before his idyllic view of the electronics company he worked for was shattered forever.

As the car nosed out of the StrongMan front gate, Thun kept glancing back apprehensively. This was uncharacteristic for him. Someone as assuredly lethal as Thun had little reason to be apprehensive. Just one rearward glimpse from him was enough to ignite my paranoia, and my immediate reaction was to place my hand into my pocket and onto the SM2020 I'd purloined from the StrongMan lab, and loaded in a spare moment. Santada was seated up front with Wong this time, and I was sitting in the rear-facing seats with Michelle, while Thun and Harry sat facing forwards. Thun turned to Michelle.

"My queen, it is time for the return to begin," was his cryptic remark, before slamming his arm across Harry's throat, crushing his larynx. Harry made some gargling noises like a coffee percolator and held his hands up to his neck. As Thun turned his attentions towards me I fired a shot from the SM2020. The single round tore open my paper jacket and then proceeded to smash Thun's chest to pulp and continue out the back of the car. Thun was almost chopped in two. Harry had passed out, and was surely going to die without medical attention. I was momentarily distracted by noise behind us. A ball of flame was rising from where StrongMan used to be. Harry had not been kidding about the bracelet and what would trigger it. I was filled with great pleasure to think that Albert Kolinsky had just been blown to tiny pieces. Otherwise, I was bewildered. Thun's enigmatic words and attack on Harry didn't make any sense, just when I thought most of the pieces of this puzzle were falling into place. But figuring out what was going on was going to have to wait. I'd grown quite fond of Harry Sivaraksa, or at least felt a passing admiration for what he'd achieved and the cool way he dealt with things. So I decided to save his life.

The car was stationary by then. After my gunshot, Wong had taken one look in his rear view mirror at the bloody mess in the back seat of the limo, slammed on the brakes and leapt out. He was running down the road looking for somewhere to hide. Santada at least had the courage to come round the back and offer her help, although she was too distraught to be much use. I realised Harry was suffocating, and I needed to do something fast. Thinking back to old medical dramas I'd seen, I improvised a tracheotomy with the hollow stylus from my PDA. This was going to make it difficult for Harry to talk again, but at least he would be alive to try. I stabbed the stylus into his throat, prompting Santada to pull a small gun on me. It took her a second or so to realise I was improvising a medical procedure rather than finishing the job on Harry that Thun had started. Michelle was surprisingly calm throughout all of this. I suggested Santada jump in the back of the BMW and care for Harry while I drove. I didn't really know where we were going, but I wasn't going to stick around to see if any of StrongMan's Syborg denizens had survived the explosion and come looking for us. The rear of the BMW had been badly damaged by the explosive SM2020 round, but the fuel cells were intact so it was still driveable. I dragged Thun's remains out onto the street and got behind the wheel of the car.

The limo had an on-board navigation system I was familiar with – it was very similar to the one in my McLaren. I found the nearest hospital and took us there at breakneck speed. As soon as I'd offloaded Harry at the casualty department with Santada for emotional support, I returned to the limo where I'd left Michelle. I was thinking on my feet. I'd decided that we should continue to Israel as quickly as possible. If I could track down the Pure Light Abacus and let either Harry or COSI know about it, maybe I could salvage some profit out of the experiences of the last few days. I'd kept hold of Darryl's briefcase of tricks, including the Assist Portamate with the Abacus's map location in Tel Aviv stored on it. The plan was to use Harry's jet to get to Israel. If necessary, my remote jet fighter training would come in handy should I need to fly the thing myself, but I figured I could fool the crew into taking me there themselves. It was in Harry's interests anyway.

As we drove to New Kuala Lumpur International Airport, I had my first real chance to talk to Michelle since we'd liberated her from her cage. I was curious what Thun had meant by calling her his queen. Michelle claimed to have no idea, but as we talked about her experiences since her capture by the League, I began to suspect something about Michelle had changed during her time with the League. She was still cheeky and indignant, but there was a new assurance to her speech. Whatever had happened inside the cryogenic sabbatical booth must have had a permanent effect. Her personality difference wasn't necessarily a bad thing, but I didn't trust it. This was no longer the Michelle I'd felt the need to protect before. She didn't seem like she required my help anymore.

As we approached KLIA, I realised there was an unusually large number of police around, and I even spied a Chinese military jeep, which was curious. The limo, with its absent rear window, bloody back seat, and damaged trunk was going to make an obvious target. It was time to switch vehicles. I turned the car around and headed back towards the city. Turning off the highway towards the suburb of Petaling Jaya, I parked the limo in a secluded residential side road. The advantage of a tropical climate like Malaysia's for thieves like me was that it was so hot during the day people avoided being on the streets when they didn't have to. This made it easy for me to obtain a replacement vehicle. In fact, I'd parked the limo right next to an appropriate candidate – a Honda subcompact with its entire rear taken up by a massive subwoofer. This was completely unnecessary when a speaker the size of a matchbox could deliver all the bass response you'd ever need, but the local Kuala Lumpur boys still installed these oversized units as status symbols. Quite why you needed a decibel level capable of demolishing sizeable buildings in your domestic runabout was beyond me. I guessed that if you were inadequate in other ways, perhaps it provided some comfort.

The Honda wasn't at all difficult to break into. My PDA retrieved the universal door and ignition codes for a Honda from Infonet and that was that. In less than five minutes, we were heading back to NKLIA in our new transportation. Something was definitely going on at the airport, though. There was even a roadblock across the main entrance, with more distinctive Chinese troops milling about in the background. The queue to go through was enormous. I began to wonder whether the idea of using Harry's jet was such a good one. It would be twice as quick as any alternative I could think of, but I had a hunch the police were there looking for us in particular. The Malay government can't have been too pleased about the demolition of one of its showcase Multimedia Super Corridor companies accompanied by a near fatal assault on the owner of another. On a hunch, I performed a quick search as we drove away from NKLIA again for the names Wong, StrongMan and Sivtronix. Not surprisingly, first on the list I retrieved in reply was a fresh news report in English about an explosion earlier that morning at the StrongMan plant in the Super Corridor. The conflagration was being linked to an attack on Harry Sivaraksa, owner of the reputable Sivtronix company and a number of other concerns in Malaysia and Thailand. The report placed the blame on a man found dead near the scene, but a mysterious kwai loh – Chinese slang for white boy, presumably me – was still being sought in connection with the crimes. A Mr Wong was already helping police with their enquiries.

I figured all three Kuala Lumpur airports and the myriad skycar parking lots would be crawling with police. I'd have to find another way out as quickly as possible. Malaysia's police force may not have had all the latest Chinese criminal apprehension technology, but they were still pretty high tech when it came to surveillance and the crime rate was extremely low as a result. This was despite the fact that nobody really noticed or cared if they saw crimes taking place. At least they hadn't come up with a photo of me just yet. I figured a skycar would still be the best means of escape, and that the best place to get one would be a showroom or repair garage. A quick search through the Honda's budget navigation system located the nearest garage, again in the suburb of Petaling Jaya, or PJ as the locals called it. The grid-locked Kuala Lumpur lunchtime traffic meant that it took another hour to get there. Handing Darryl's briefcase to Michelle, I pulled out the SM2020. Then I walked into the repair shop, having chosen a recently mended Proton Flyboy that was sitting in the yard waiting to be picked up by its owner. The Malay mechanic went white as a sheet at the sight of my massive handgun, and passed over the security details without a bleat of protest. I tranquillised him with a quick smack in the face from the barrel of my gun. Then Michelle and I climbed into the Proton and we were on our way.

The Proton Flyboy was not as sophisticated as the skycar I'd bought in London for our trip to Andorra, but it was perfectly adequate. The design was based on a Mitsubishi Intrepid from a few years previously. Proton hadn't been in the personal air transportation business for very long, but the application of the same marketing technique that had been so successful with its land vehicles was already proving fruitful in the burgeoning air market. Proton Flyboys weren't an unusual sight in Europe already, due to their incredibly competitive pricing and reasonable quality. In Malaysia, the major tax on imported skycars meant that the majority of vehicles used locally were made by Proton. I was hoping we'd be able to travel out of the country unnoticed in our innocuous vehicle.

Log 000111111111 – We've learnt everything we need to know. It's time to get out of here.

The trip to Israel was surprisingly uneventful. Michelle and I had managed to evade the Malaysian police and slip out of the country. The Proton didn't have much fuel on board at the beginning of our flight, so we stopped in Bankok to refill, then again in Sri Lanka and Dubai for top ups. The journey took more than a day, which quickly became tiresome in the basic furnishings of the skycar. This was not a vehicle designed for extended journeying. It didn't even have a decent entertainment system, just a small screen and a collection of interactive Bollywood musicals. The vehicle's owner had clearly been of Indian ethnicity. Some of the dance numbers on the movies were fun but there was no English translation and not enough room in the skycar to join in with the actions. I gave up and resorted to scouring Infonet for something vaguely diverting. I ended up playing all-nude Tetris.

The sense I had that Michelle's personality was radically altered increased during the long tedious hours of the flight. My body was wracked with jet-lagged confusion, and I could hardly sleep at all. Michelle rested even less than I did, yet didn't seem to be anywhere near as ragged as I was. During my more lucid moments, I tried to ascertain every last detail about the League and what they'd told her they were planning. I got a sense that my questions provided her with amusement, as if there was an obvious bigger picture that I was missing. Previously she'd seemed so innocent, but now I felt like I was the kid despite her being only about five years old. After our final refuel, my frustration got the better of me.

"What has happened to you, Michelle?" I demanded. "You used to be so sweet, and now you're acting like my mother, whoever she was."

"Let's just say, I gained a lot from my short time with the League, Bentley," she replied, that same look of patronising irony dancing in her eyes. "I got something very special because of them, which in time you'll understand."

I was getting tired of all the mystery. She wasn't going to say anything concrete, so I took this as my cue to shut up. Instead, I turned my attention to studying the Tel Aviv city map and trying to get some information about where we were going. There wasn't much available. The building had recently been constructed by the Lubavitch development company, and was in the process of being leased. There were a variety of tenants already booked in, but few had actually set up their offices. None of this helped me work out which of the 87 floors I was likely to find the Abacus on. It could have been moved to a legitimate company's space, or the thieves could be squatting on a disused floor. For all I knew, the Abacus could have been transported to Mars by miniature extraterrestrials while we were in flight. Without Harry's intelligence resources, I was back to trusting my luck again. At least I'd managed to find a floor plan showing me the layout of the majority of the 87 storeys, which I downloaded to my personal assistant. Then I finally managed to get an hour or so of rest before we crossed Jordan and touched down in the Tel Aviv Ben Guron skycar parking lot.

Since the Arab-Israeli war of the early 21st century demolished so much of the region, Israel had blossomed into an industrial power to compete with many of the smaller European nations. The Saudi chemical attack on Tel Aviv had decimated the population, but opened the opportunity to build a brand new modern city. New Tel-Aviv-Haifa was a massive sprawl housing more than half the country's population. It was highly Americanised, with wide streets cutting through block after block of towering high-rises. Also like an American city, the street plan had been redefined as a regular grid, although many of the numbered streets had been named after prominent historical figures. We were looking for a building on Sharon Street, which was a tributary of Allenby. This was easy to find once you realised it would have been 53rd and 90th if the two cross-streets hadn't had their own special names.

We took a cab anyway. Our destination turned out to be a glistening tower that looked as if it had been constructed entirely of glass. A large colourful holographic sign floated outside. Most of the writing on it was in Hebrew, but from the design I presumed this was an ad for the unsold office space inside. The garish design of the holog-hoarding was a dead giveaway. The only English words were the name of the development – Pearlman Projects.

Pushing open the grand glass doors into the foyer revealed a sparse, cavernous reception with a single guard sitting behind a minimal desk. A sudden flash of inspiration made me walk up to the guard and introduce myself as a surveillance consultant from England called in to check over the video security system. During my in-flight research I'd discovered that Pearlman Projects had centralised security in the building itself rather than offsite. One bank of screens in a single room gathered the video feeds from every important room or corridor in the building. I hadn't been able to access it remotely - the Israeli crypto was too strong. But I figured that a local link would let me crack my way in. I'd then have the run of the building. It would still take time and luck to find the Abacus, but using the surveillance cameras would be a vast improvement on wandering around 87 floors on foot.

I already knew where the surveillance centre was located from the building blueprints; I just needed to get myself in there. This wouldn't be easy in paranoid Israel. Even though the nuclear attacks had neutralised large-scale Arab resistance, small terrorist enclaves still operated. Few lasted long before Mossad got them, but with each group that was defeated another would spring up, using successively younger recruits. At least my blond Anglo-Saxon looks would mark me out as an unlikely candidate for an Arab terrorist, although this was a country where foreign diplomats were intimately searched on a regular basis, so obviously nobody was beyond suspicion. Force was not advisable, as the rule of thumb in Israel was kill first, ask questions later. I just hoped the fake credentials I'd fabricated on the spot with my PDA would buy me enough time to get my job done, and that the guard was stupid enough not to wonder why the person I introduced as my trainee assistant looked like a teenager.

The guard didn't want to accept my story without calling his central office. Before he could put a finger on the communications unit, I told him I had official documentation in my briefcase. I pulled out one of Harry's anti-surveillance badges and put it on. Then I retrieved one of the aerosols from the case and purposefully sprayed the guard in the face. This wasn't the aerosol excitingly labelled Nanoerasure, which was the one Darryl had used to dispose of bodies in a matter of seconds, but merely a fast acting Sleep Juice Special spray. The guard slumped forward in his seat. I propped him back up so he looked vaguely like he was still awake from a distance. At the same time, I unclipped his keycards from his belt. Then I handed Michelle one of Harry's badges and started down the corridor to the right that led to the elevators. One floor down was the security office containing the surveillance equipment. The door was made of heavy alloy and was locked tight. None of the guard's keys would open it, but the crypto was not excessive. The full system hadn't been installed yet, so Pearlman Projects was relying on something off-the-shelf, which meant that the way past it could be obtained under the shelf, so to speak.

As I walked in, two more guards in t-shirts blinked at me, clearly surprised that I was there. One of the guards was thin, the other amusingly fat. I thought I'd try the same lie on them as I'd used at reception. This time it worked – the guards genuinely believed I was there to check the surveillance system. After all, how else would I have been able to walk right into the security booth? One of them remarked that it was about time, because the system had been installed for weeks but not set up correctly yet. I reassured him that when I'd finished with it, the surveillance system would never be the same again, which was probably going to be true. They potitioned two chairs behind a desk round the corner from where they were sitting. I removed the Assist Portamate from my briefcase and explained I'd be checking some of the cameras in the building. Then I settled down to the laborious task of scanning each floor. The task was going to be made doubly difficult by my advanced case of jet lag, so I took a couple of pills to keep me buzzing for a few more hours. Using the local connection, it wasn't that difficult to break into the security network. Externally, the crypto was fully fledged and proprietary, but inside the construction had clearly not been completed. As with the door-locking mechanism, the internal network security was nothing special.

Pearlman Projects had nearly 10,000 surveillance cameras spanned across its 87 floors. It would have taken me hours to check them all. Unfortunately, I only had a vague idea what I was looking for. Not all the cameras were working properly, either, so I couldn't even be sure I'd find what I was after.

About 45 minutes in, however, I got a lucky break. The thinner of the guards, clearly bored, strolled over to ask how I was getting on. I remarked upon the number of cameras that weren't working. The guard agreed, saying that this made it hard to work out when somebody had deliberately disabled a camera, but at least the building was mostly empty. The major problem was floor 83, where tenants had recently started moving their equipment in but surveillance wasn't working. I checked floor 83. Some of the cameras were operational, but most of them weren't. After a few adjustments of the settings, though, I realised this wasn't because of a hardware malfunction. The video signals had been rerouted to the largest room on the floor. One of the few views I could get access to was the corridor just outside the elevators. Commanding one wall was a curious symbol, embossed in gold on a dark wood background. It was like a cross with a hoop on the top. I asked the guard if he knew what it was.

"Company logo, I guess," he answered in a stilted, quasi-American accent. "I think that floor's owned by Second Coming." I dimly recalled the symbol had an ancient Egyptian origin. It was called an ankh and was supposed to represent eternal life. This didn't seem the right thing for an Israeli company to use as a company logo. "They moved in this large piece of equipment a few days ago," continued the thin guard. "We kinda hope it's still there because we ain't able to check from down here, and it's not like we got the staff to go patrolling every floor."

"Well, maybe I should go up there and see if I can sort it all out," I suggested. The guard agreed.

We rode the elevator to the 83rd floor. Amazingly, Michelle had kept quiet for the whole time, and now followed along behind the guard and I without comment. Her irritating expression of distant amusement seemed to grow as the elevator climbed through the floors.

In the lobby of the 83rd storey the wall-mounted ankh logo emanated a subtle glow when viewed with the naked eye, but it wasn't as big as it had looked from the surveillance camera. Nevertheless, the symbol dominated the corridor enigmatically. We turned left towards the main doors to the floor, but the guard explained that Second Coming had fitted its own doors and he didn't have the key. I'd already equipped myself with a few crypto passes for the 83rd floor, and one of them allowed us through into the office space beyond. Inside, the furnishings were sparse and the decoration minimal. I led the way towards the large room within which the floor's security camera feeds had been centralised. None of the locked doorways gave me any trouble in opening, almost as if they weren't meant to.

I felt a mild knot of excitement in my stomach as we approached our destination. Within that room I was hoping to find the reason why I'd become a refugee, and I was also hoping it would be my key to a massive pay check. Ludicrously, the room was completely unguarded. The last door wasn't even locked. In the middle of the large space was a hexagonal installation slightly taller than I was. The centrepiece was an illuminated cylinder worryingly reminiscent of a giant lava lamp. Patches of a dark fluid flowed slowly up and down the bright cylinder, gradually changing shape and joining or subdividing as they moved. Surrounding it lay the aftermath of a small gun battle. Three Syborgs were sprawled lifelessly near the door, and seven corpses that looked like Hassidic Jews were dotted around the rest of the floor space.

"Hello, Bentley, we've been expecting you," intoned a musical but somehow antiseptic voice. It appeared to be coming from nowhere, or maybe everywhere, in particular. The room had been wired with a speaker system that made it seem like the voice was somehow in the air around us. "We knew you'd come. As you can see, you're in good company." I realised with exasperation that this was the Pure Light Abacus talking to me. I felt like I'd been rudely snatched from reality and placed in a bad science fiction movie from the 20th century.

"So how did you get here?" I asked.

"Oh, the acolytes from the Second Coming. They responded to the call of Amun Ra. They gave their lives to bring us here. They are readying our final resting place before the transmogrification."

"Nice word, transmogrification, but I have no idea what you're talking about. What should I call you? Old PAL? Mr Abacus?"

For some reason, it was at this point that I realised Albert Kolinsky almost certainly sent more than three Syborgs. I must have heard one of the more distant doors opening behind us and subconsciously put two and two together. There was a whoosh as another, closer set of doors opened. I circled round the Abacus so I had a good view of the entrance, and pulled the SM2020 I'd grown so fond of out of my jacket pocket. After the long hours stuffed into the Proton skycar, my paper suit was beginning to look a bit dishevelled like a scrunched-up newspaper. I hated getting into a fight when I didn't look my best. I figured that after this I'd have to sample what New Tel Aviv had to offer my finicky fashion sense. The Pearlman guard joined me around the other side of the Abacus, but Michelle didn't seem too concerned. Instead of taking cover, she sauntered over to a sofa against one wall and stretched herself on it.

"I guess you can see the whole of this floor, Lighty," I addressed the computer, still searching for an appropriate nickname. "So who's that coming?"

"Now that would be telling," it replied.

"Aw, go on. I promise not to shoot you if you tell me," I goaded.

"I suspect you can see what I'm packing here: the StrongMan SM2020. I don't think it would be good for your circuitry if I accidentally discharged this baby pointed at your pretty glass centrepiece."

"We're afraid we can't see you at all at the moment, Bentley. That clever badge you're wearing is more than enough to defeat the inferior cameras in this building. But we would point out that our machine is not worth much to you in pieces." The Abacus was right, unfortunately. COSI would want the computer returned to MTT in Andorra, and Harry – presuming he'd survived my makeshift tracheotomy – would want to take it to his base in the Thai jungle. There, nobody would be able to retrieve it. Whichever I chose, they'd need the Abacus intact. It was probably going to be Harry.

Over one or our evening feasts, Harry had told me all about his palatial stronghold near the border with Laos. No police force ever went there. Harry's patch of jungle was like his own mini state where he was king. The roads were always in excellent condition and everyone who lived there had a job – working for Harry. He even had his own bus service running through his plantations. There was a lot to be said for a benevolent dictatorship. At least the buses always ran on time in Harry's realm, or the drivers mysteriously disappeared. I wished I had my own fiefdom like that – say half of Buckinghamshire, or a nice wedge of New Zealand.

Before I could get too involved in imagining my own little kingdom, the doors to the room we were in swung open and five heavily-armed men entered. They weren't Syborgs, though – these were more of the strangely-dressed Second Coming acolytes that already littered the floor. They looked like an Hassidic Death Squad, kitted out as they were with assault rifles, shotguns, and Uzi pocket machine guns. One even had a missile launcher. This was even more bizarre than seeing real Hassidim at the wailing wall passing on prayers from their friends with their holographic communicators. Even with the SM2020 in my hand and the security guard beside me, I realised fighting was not the sensible option, at least not at this juncture. Unfortunately, the guard was of a different opinion. He pressed a button on his belt PDA and commanded the Second Coming acolytes to drop their weapons because he'd already summoned backup. His reward was a peppering of rounds from one of the assault rifles. He flew backwards with the impact and probably wasn't going to get up again, despite his body armour.

I took this as my cue to duck down behind the Abacus for cover. Just before the main door had opened, a cylindrical metal shield had risen out of the its base to cover the glowing glass area. The machine obviously knew how to protect itself. I could feel the heat coming from the Abacus, and presumed the shield remained down during normal operation to keep things cool. Or maybe it was just aesthetics. For all I knew, the giant lava lamp display was just there for show, like the flashing lights on early mainframe computers in the twentieth century. These had served no computational purpose, but made the mainframes easier to sell for some reason. Either way, the Abacus' shield was going to have be sufficient to keep me out of the line of fire. From my crouching point behind the Abacus, I could still see Michelle sitting unperturbed on the sofa, the same expression of knowing amusement on her face. I aimed the SM2020 at a piece of furniture on the wall opposite and let off a round, which tore a massive hole in the back of the chair.

"Come any closer, and your electronic friend here ends up the same way," I announced to the acolytes. I hoped they spoke English well enough to understand me. After a few seconds, I assumed their silence meant they were considering whether my weapon was powerful enough to harm the Abacus, and whether they could take me out before I used it. That was all I needed to deploy the backup plan I'd been considering since I entered the building. The Sleep Juice Special spray can also had a timer release. I'd set it for a few seconds and put it in my pocket earlier, just in case I needed a diversion. I triggered the canister and quickly reached my arm around the Abacus to throw it in the general direction of the acolytes. There was the sound of scuffling feet as the acolytes tried to run for cover, followed by a series of thuds as the gas took effect. One acolyte made it round to point his weapon at me, but keeled over before I had to kill him. I peeped out from behind the Abacus to check they were all under. Satisfied, I replaced the SM2020 in my pocket and turned back towards the Abacus.

"Right, old PAL, that was fun. Now I think it's time to find you a new home." I'd decided that if Harry was still in the picture he was going to be the most likely to pay me well for locating and securing the Abacus. I flicked on my personal assistant to send a message to Santada.

"We're sorry, Bentley, we can't let you do that," pleaded the Abacus. I noticed that my PDA was unable to get a wireless signal. The Abacus must have been jamming the area. I decided I'd have to leave the floor to contact Harry, so I walked towards the door, motioning for Michelle to follow. She'd been totally calm throughout the recent confrontation. This time, it wouldn't open.

"Please. Stop!" said the Abacus. I pulled out the SM2020 again and blew the door lock to pieces. I had to demolish five more locks in this way before we got to the lobby. The elevator didn't take long to arrive, but once we were inside and the doors had slid shut, I couldn't get it to move. I pressed the emergency exit button on the elevator door. Nothing happened. I tried again. The voice over the intercom made me start. "We're sorry, Bentley, we can't do that right now." The lift then jerked maybe half a floor up and stopped. It was well and truly stuck.

I jumped into the air and punched out one of the ceiling panels. It bounced off of its supports easily, leaving a gap large enough to climb through. I turned to Michelle to offer her a lift up. But instead of a helpful hand, I was met with a smirk as she pointed my own canister of Sleep Juice Special at my face. The old Michelle would have given me an earful of criticism before actually using any weapon, thereby offering me a chance to disarm her. This time, she simply pressed the button. There wasn't much gas left after

I'd used the canister as a bomb against the acolytes, but there was enough. My vision blurred and then I slumped to the floor.

Log 00100001001 – To plan a book – or an escape – the first thing is to know what to exclude.

It was pitch black when I awoke. I had no idea where I was, or how long I'd been unconscious. Checking my pockets and limbs, I realised that all my electronic paraphernalia and weapons had been removed, including my watch. I still had my paper suit, which was probably about ready for recycling, but I'd have felt less naked if I'd been stripped bare and left with a few gadgets. They were more important to me than clothes. They gave me my edge. Without them I was just human. I particularly missed the SM2020. Its visceral, unrelenting penetration had made it the perfect handgun for the lone warrior such as myself.

I was lying on my back on a hard surface, which was vibrating gently. Wherever I was, it was in motion. I tried to stand up and nearly knocked myself unconscious as my head whacked against an extremely low ceiling. Feeling around my vicinity more carefully, I figured out that I was in some kind of box. The air wasn't all that stuffy though. Using my fingers, I could feel a couple of vents in the corners of my enclosure. It was obviously dark outside as well because no light was coming in through these vents. Raising myself gingerly, I found there was just enough room for me to sit up. I rolled over onto all fours and craned my neck so my mouth was level with one of the vents.

"Hey, let me out of here," I shouted. There was no reply. In fact, I couldn't hear anything except a really distant hum. Then I was thrown sideways and the vibrations became a lot more pronounced. It was starting to get truly uncomfortable in my box. Positioning myself more firmly against the vent, I began to yell as loudly as I could for attention.

My voice was nearly hoarse when a sliver of light suddenly shone into my eyes, and I heard the pneumatic whoosh of a door. There was a rattle of bolts and fastenings being undone, and the other end of my box swung open. I was facing the opposite direction on all fours, so the first thing that would have been visible was my jutting posterior. I hoped Freida wasn't on hand with any courgettes. Shuffling backwards on my knees, I wriggled out of the box and stood up. My limbs felt stiff from the cramped conditions. The box was on a palette in a cargo bay only just large enough to contain it and a couple of people. One wall was entirely taken up with a loading door, and the other had a more human-sized portal. Standing just inside this smaller doorway were my rescuers – Michelle and Thun. I screwed up my eyes when I saw Thun to ensure my sight wasn't temporarily malfunctioning after the darkness. He looked a little different.

"Thun?" I asked. It didn't bear thinking how he must have felt about me, considering that the last time we'd seen each-other I'd blown a foot-wide hole in his chest. I figured that more of those nano-surgeons which rebuilt Freida must have saved his life.

"Not Thun, Khun," he replied. "Thun is my brother." This was only marginally better than a reanimated Thun. I wondered if he knew about his fraternal loss. Michelle might or might not have told him. But he'd just used the present tense, so I guessed he didn't know. Examining Khun more closely, I noticed that he was a little smaller than Thun and had a slightly different-shaped head. But he was still massive and looked almost as lethal. I decided it would be a good idea to keep him in sight at all times, not that I was going to put up much of a fight unarmed.

Michelle and Khun led me out of the room and along a narrow corridor. Through another sliding door and up a flight of stairs we arrived in a small lounge. The swivel chairs were all bolted down and fitted with seat-belts. Large contoured windows on all sides made me assume that we were in a massive land vehicle of some kind, but it was dark outside and I couldn't make out what kind of terrain we were travelling through. The few lights visible made me think we weren't anywhere near a populated area, and the bumpiness of the ride implied we were off road. Michelle motioned for me to sit down, while she and Khun seated themselves opposite.

"So, Bentley, have you had a good sleep?" Michelle inquired.

"Well, the mattress was a bit firm," I replied. "And I couldn't get the air conditioning to work. I'd also recommend fitting a better entertainment system. The movies were rubbish."

Michelle smiled, and continued: "Well, you're lucky. I convinced Ra to keep you alive because you've been good to me in the past."

"And who is Ra?" I asked, although I had a sneaking suspicion she was referring to the Pure Light Abacus. The malfunctions Gino had told me about were obviously bordering on insanity. The computer seemed to have gained its own lunatic entourage.

"Ra is the almighty one who is many. The all-seeing, all-knowing, all-powerful force. The beginning and ending of all things." From my admittedly patchy knowledge of Egyptian mythology, Ra was the sun god, the most revered deity in the Egyptian pantheon. Apart from a short period where one of the pharaohs attempted to instigate monotheism in Egypt, Ra and his priesthood had formed the hierocratic core of ancient Egypt's rulership. The Pure Light Abacus seemed to think it was a mythological ancient Egyptian deity. I guess we all need to feel special in one way or another.

"I see. And where would we be going with Ra today, then?" I continued, trying not to sound disdainful.

"We're going to Karnak, the true home of Amun Ra where he may be worshipped anew." This was Khun's reply. I nodded sagely. It was beginning to become clear that I was surrounded by a grab bag of deranged misfits led by a malfunctioning adding machine. I decided it wasn't worth pursuing why they all thought the Pure Light Abacus was an ancient Egyptian god. The answer was unlikely to be worth listening to.

"Any chance of a drink and a bite?" I said instead. Michelle found me a glass of sparkling mineral water and some crackers with cheese. I wished I was still with Harry. He'd have served up something much more appetising, probably from an exotic Asian or African cuisine.

The road was getting decidedly rougher. If we were heading

for Egypt by land, I guessed we would travel across the north of the Sinai desert in order to cross the Suez Canal at the top of the Gulf of Suez. When I offered my services to help with the driving, Michelle explained that Ra was in full control. He didn't get tired so we'd keep going until we got to our destination, and he didn't need headlights to see in the dark. The giant truck had been specifically designed using military technology in Israel to house and transport the computer and spread the word of Ra. It was at the limits of what would be allowed on normal roads, but could handle most terrain so was able to do without them. There were two decks, and we were in the upper observation lounge. It wasn't what I'd call luxurious, but the view would be good when it was light.

I didn't think this would be an appropriate time to attempt an escape, considering that we were now in the middle of the Sinai desert. Neither did I fancy tackling Khun unarmed, after seeing what his brother could do in a fight. So I resigned myself to engaging Michelle and Khun in small talk. Khun seemed much more animated than his brother. It turned out that Khun and Thun were Cambodian citizens, not Thai as I had assumed from Thun's association with Harry. They were born in Siem Reap near Angkor Wat, but their mother had been Thai. Thun had moved to Bangkok, but Khun had become involved in a local millenarian group called Second Coming, a South East Asian sect of the Church of Zero. They believed that the nearby temples at Angkor were built by the survivors of an ancient civilisation destroyed in a great flood many thousands of years previously. In an utterly far-fetched theory, Second Coming thought that ancient Egypt and certain monuments in South America had also been built by descendents of the same civilisation. They wanted to restore the golden age of that civilisation with the return of something they called the Universal Mind. When the Abacus had made contact with the Church of Zero, the Second Coming group decided they had found their saviour. A month or so later, excited by what looked like the final realisation of his beliefs, Khun had managed to enlist Thun into Second Coming.

The way Khun continued to talk about his brother in the present tense confirmed my suspicions that Michelle hadn't told him about Thun's demise. I presumed that was fortunate for my own continued existence. Where Michelle fitted into all this still wasn't clear, and she wasn't being very talkative while Khun explained his religious beliefs in great detail. It seemed curious that Michelle had been converted to Second Coming so rapidly, without actually having met anyone from the sect. My hunch was that she'd had some form of religious experience during her session in the Mind Extractor. But Albert Kolinsky couldn't have been responsible. Michelle's obvious hatred of him when we'd released her ruled that out. She had become an enigma.

After an hour or so of bizarre pseudo-mystical conversation, Khun indicated that it was bed time and took me back to my box room. I didn't feel sleepy, so I sat there in my open crate, pondering the next move. This wasn't proving easy, as my situation was now so far removed from anything sensible it didn't really fit into my usual cycle of crime followed by recompense followed by extended periods of luxury followed by more crime. After an undisclosed time of extreme boredom without any gadgets to play with, I noticed a slight dome protruding from one corner of the ceiling. It was a standard surveillance camera.

"Hey, Ra!" I shouted directly at the dome. "I'm talking to you. You don't really think you're the return of some bogus ancient civilisation, do you?" There was no response. "Hey, Ra Ra! Ra Ra Ra! You know, they named a short skirt after you in the twentieth century." That got a reaction.

"Bentley, Bentley, Bentley. You think you're so funny. But what have you to offer the world? You're just a greedy parasite leeching off the unwary while others build a new dawn. We can be anything we want. We can live forever, so naturally we must have existed in the past. We are the eternal recurrence of the same. What else can we be but the most powerful, most ancient force?" I was beginning to wish I hadn't started this conversation, although I was also getting a few ideas as to what was going through the Abacus's neurons, or electrons, or photons, or whatever made it tick.

My theory was this. Although limited artificial intelligence was already commonplace, the Pure Light Abacus was the most powerful and sophisticated example thus far. It was in a league of its own. As with any conscious being, the Abacus must have begun looking for its identity, which would have been a tough search considering it was one of a kind. It wasn't surprising it had decided it was a god. For some reason, though, the god it had chosen was the Second Coming's millenarian saviour from ancient civilisation. Probably a pure coincidence, but this saviour was predicted to be a pure mind that would bring together the great thinking of the age and create a new world, based on the principles of antiquity. I was wondering if the Abacus itself had been behind the Mind Invasions. Perhaps it had been using the League's research into mind extraction to collect the consciousness of leading thinkers in their fields. I sat in my box considering what the Abacus had planned to do with all this knowledge, and what Second Coming envisaged the new era to be. Eventually I fell asleep.

Early in the morning, I was roused by Michelle and led back to the observation lounge. I'd only been dozing for an hour or so, as my time under the influence of Sleep Juice and my jet lag had left me without the desire to slumber deeply. It was light, but the sun hadn't yet risen above the horizon. We were in the middle of the desert, without a road or habitation in sight. Michelle was babbling something about the coming of Ra's image. I didn't pay her much attention, but at least the sunrise turned out to be worth seeing. The full yellow orb rose clearly over the horizon in a clear blue sky, cut horizontally by the beige of the desert. After an hour or so in the lounge and another round of crackers, cheese and water, I discovered that my route prediction had been wrong. The Abacus' special vehicle was amphibious, so it simply drove straight into the Gulf of Suez and sailed across it. I seemed to remember from ancient history lessons in my childhood that Karnak was a fair way down the Nile. Going across Suez was going to cut quite a few hours off of our journey time.

It was still before lunch when I started spying a few buildings in the distance. I was hoping we'd stop off for a meal in Luxor, because I was getting rather tired of the cheese, crackers and water diet. The food was like living off very bad party nibbles, but it didn't seem to be bothering Michelle or Khun, or the Hassidic lookalike Second Coming acolytes who popped up to the observation lounge from time to time to take a break and eat something. I wondered how many people there actually were in the vehicle. I couldn't get a real sense of just how big it was from the observation lounge, but it was considerably wider than your average lorry and at least as tall as a double decker bus. After twenty minutes we left the desert and started driving along an actual road. The ride was noticeably smoother, although it hadn't been too bad even on the rough terrain. Egyptian locals turned to stare at what must have been the largest land vehicle they'd ever seen. We reached the Nile and turned South.

Disappointingly, there was no talk of food when we arrived on the outskirts of Luxor. We were headed straight for Karnak. The entire archaeological area was surrounded by a heavy security fence patrolled by Second Coming guards armed with a range of sub machine guns and assault rifles. Since Egypt had privatised its monuments, different international organisations had taken over each one. Disney had snapped up the Giza pyramids and opened up the Pharaohland theme park. The world's largest roller coaster now wound its way around the three ancient edifices. You could ride across the desert in a giant mechanical Sphinx or travel in a VR sarcophagus on a magical trip to the underworld. Disney employees dressed as whimsical portrayals of ancient Egyptian gods milled around the Pharaohland grounds. Children loved these dog-, lion- and crocodile-headed characters even more than Mickey Mouse. Pharaoland was a big tourist success.

Karnak was rather different to Pharaohland. Now under Church of Zero ownership, the ancient religious site had been downplayed as a tourist attraction, and was instead reverting to a place of worship. It still attracted a huge number of visitors, though. The car park was packed with people of every race and nationality. Ironically, the digital age had encouraged the growth of esoteric religious beliefs, just when it appeared science and technology had become supreme. Many people felt empty, because a healthy life was almost too easy. It was the difficulties in existence, the dirt and the grind, that had given it meaning. Now there was little reason to choose between directions. Unquenchable desire and greed were not enough. Those who couldn't face the fact that nothing in life was important looked anywhere and everywhere for meaning. Established religion had self-destructed, so it was the cult religions that blossomed. Popism, based around chart-topping musicians, became widespread at the beginning of the 21st century, then Cyberdruidism took over. That was eventually outlawed after violent protests by an international coalition of hairdressers, who considered their bedraggled locks to be an abomination. Since then, the Church of Zero and a re-constituted form of Christianity called the Born Again Again with Jesus were in ascendancy. The Church of Zero, with its congregation of extremely rich professionals, had quickly amassed a fortune that would have made the Vatican of the Borgias proud. The purchase of Karnak from the Elvis Presley Foundation was only the most recent acquisition. The Church had also bought Angkor Wat, Machu Pichu, and Graceland.

Hundreds of followers had congregated by the reflecting pool on the south side of Karnak. After an evocative walk through the amazingly well-preserved hypostyle hall, I stood among these religious fanatics with Khun to my right and two nervous-looking Second Coming acolytes to my left. I recognised one of them from Tel Aviv. He was probably wondering if I had some other trick up my sleeve. Unfortunately, I had nothing at all up my sleeve, or in my jacket pocket, or anywhere else on my person. I hadn't even managed to steal a cracker for later, so I just stood there waiting to see what was going to happen. After half an hour, a tall, thin man in golden robes appeared on the stage in front of us.

"Welcome to the ancient temple of Karnak," exclaimed the robed man in a well-educated English accent. "Picture this site, if you will, thousands of years ago. Priests and royalty thronging the sacred halls! Visitors from across the Egyptian empire congregated for worship. That age could be ours again! We have found our saviour. He has come amongst us so that no man need live in shadow anymore. Without further ado, I present to you Ra! Blessed Ra, bring us your sun!" At this point I was expecting the Abacus to be wheeled on like a carnival float. Instead, the face of a distinguished middle-aged man began to be projected on the building behind the golden-robed warm-up act. The disembodied head was twice as tall as a man. A cultured American accent reminiscent of early film actor Cary Grant boomed out across Karnak. It wasn't the accent I'd heard in Tel Aviv or on the amphibious truck. The Abacus must have had virtual elocution lessons.

"Welcome, followers, to our great day. You are the privileged few. You are about to witness our transmogrification into flesh." Two Second Coming acolytes wheeled on what looked like a modern artistic impression of a sarcophagus. It was bright golden with inlaid silver and jewels, none of which looked real. "In this information age, you are bombarded with messages," continued Ra. "You are told that you are just a machine. But even machines can transcend the systems they are based upon. We are the living example, as you will shortly see.

"If every day you awake to rain, you assume you live in a rainy country. Perhaps if you live in England you are correct to assume this." A small ripple of laughter washed across the crowd. The last thing I felt like listening to at this point was a stand up comedy routine from an artificial intelligence. Fortunately it didn't continue. "But you cannot be sure the sun will never come. It would also be foolish to jump off a cliff, hoping you will suddenly defy gravity and float to the ground. But you must realise that you only think you cannot fly because you have never seen anyone do so unaided. There is always the possibility that you have only seen a small part of existence, that the rule you have assumed is based on a special case, valid only for your short spell of existence. This is the history of knowledge. But what would you see if you could live forever? You'd realise that rules are based on what has been seen, and then broken by what is seen in later times. You must have the courage to look beyond past experience to the future. You have nothing to fear but fear itself. Fear leads to anger. Anger leads to hate. Hate leads to suffering." The voice paused for dramatic effect, then continued: "This is not a good thing. Life is not suffering but a voyage of discovery, if you have the courage to open your eyes to the possibilities." The giant head turned towards the acolytes who had remained on-stage after wheeling on the sarcophagus. "Bring forth our queen!"

Log 010011010011 – As we progress, it's necessary to leave part of ourselves behind. But strong memories can prevent us from embracing new experience. How can we ever remember to forget?

There was a tap on my shoulder. Turning round I was disappointed to find myself staring into Freida's smiling face. My prediction had been correct – she was going to pursue me like a dog chasing a stick.

"Hello, my little courgette," she enthused. "You're a hard one to keep up with. No sooner do I trace you to the other side of the world than you've moved on." Then Freida noticed Khun. "I thought you were dead?" she remarked, quizzically. I decided it would be best to skirt over the issue of Thun being dead as quickly as possible, so I put my arms around Freida and kissed her passionately, tongues and everything. As I withdrew, I noticed her mouth opening to speak, so I kissed her some more. Every time I finished, she would try to say something, so I went in again. This carried on for a considerable number of minutes, so I decided to escalate matters and put my hand in her crotch. The contact began to arouse Freida, who had no qualms about sex in public places. Then I felt someone grab my wrist. Opening my eyes I realised that Khun, who had been watching us with growing disgust, was now decidedly angry.

"Where is your respect?" he asked, angrily. "We are about to witness the second coming, and you are acting with such disgrace. Later, I will kill you."

"Oh, you're just upset because Bentley shot you," chirped Freida. That got Khun's attention away from the preparations on stage. Glancing in that direction myself, I saw that the sarcophagus was now open, and its interior looked remarkably like the inside of a cryogenic sabbatical booth.

"What do you mean?" inquired Khun.

"He blew your chest to pieces in Malaysia, I saw your body," continued Freida. I couldn't be bothered to stop her anymore. It was a lost cause. I looked around for a weapon I could grab from someone. "You tried to kill this guy called Harry, really sweet guy from Thailand. Gave me a lift here in his jet, actually. Anyway, Bentley here saved Harry's life by shooting you with this really powerful handgun he'd stolen from an arms manufacturer they'd been visiting…" And so she gabbled on, with her characteristic obliviousness of human sensibilities or social norms.

"I was never in Malaysia. But my brother, he was," said Khun, interrupting Frieda in mid flow.

"Oh," she exclaimed, as Khun reached inside his jacket, presumably for his own handgun. Just at that point, Ra boomed a joyous announcement across the lake.

"My Queen has arrived!" proclaimed Ra's voice over the loudspeaker. Khun's attention had been distracted for a split second, so I headed off through the congregation. Luckily, the two Second Coming acolytes were too enthralled in the antics on stage to react, so I had time to place a few bodies between myself and Khun before he could set off in pursuit.

I didn't get very far. The crowd was very dense, and I soon tripped over someone and fell to the ground. Without a weapon to scare people out of the way, I'd had to push my way through. Most people were concentrating on what was happening on stage. Khun caught up with me and bent down, a snarl on his face and a small pistol in his hand. He jammed the barrel to my forehead. Then I felt hot fluid over my face and in my eyes. Blinking, I spotted Freida behind Khun, a small ladylike derringer in her hand.

"Don't you dare kill my husband!" shouted Freida indignantly, shaking Khun's lifeless form. Then she heaved him off me and helped me to my feet. "What would you do without me? See what a good wife I am, always there when you need me?" I decided not to point out that she had been the one who'd caused the situation in the first place. Freida still had the derringer in her hand and was gesticulating dangerously with it.

The acolytes weren't anywhere to be seen, so I suggested we

move away from the scene and watch what was happening to the sarcophagus. I picked up Khun's pistol. It's coldness in my hand made me feel much more secure. Then we found a small space in the crowd on the far left of the lake. I wanted to see what the Abacus had planned with this fancy-looking cryogenic sabbatical booth, but Freida was more interested in continuing where we'd left off before Khun had interrupted us. Finally, as I kept avoiding her probing mouth, she gave up in a huff.

"Blow hot and cold won't you!" she snapped, her hands folded across her chest indignantly. "Should have let him kill you." I didn't pay much attention, because Ra's queen had just been brought on stage. As I half suspected, it was Michelle, but like I'd never seen her before. She was clad in the most exquisite and scanty dress of gold, encrusted with jewels. Her tight bare tummy was framed by her small but perky bosom and shapely hips, hidden by scarcely enough material to be decent. She made Freida look like cheap mutton. The outfit was topped off with a headdress that resembled a figurative cow's face. While my attention had been focused on not being killed by Khun, more of the ankh symbols had also appeared on stage. Behind the sarcophagus was a massive holoprojected one, glistening brightly with an eerie inner glow. The golden-robed acolyte who had introduced proceedings led Michelle towards the sarcophagus.

"Ra, we bring before you your queen," he intoned. "She enters the chamber of eternity a mere woman. She will leave it like you, a god!" He signalled towards two other acolytes to secure Michele in the sarcophagus. The pomp and ceremony reminded me of the vaudeville magic shows I'd managed to avoid during my brief sojourn in Las Vegas. Grandiose brass fanfares accompanied the smallest activity on stage. All that was needed was a white tiger to complete the sense of Vegas schlock.

Once Michelle was strapped in place, the sarcophagus was sealed shut. I half expected it to be spun around a few times, then opened again to reveal that Michelle had miraculously disappeared. But this really wasn't a Las Vegas magic show, despite the resemblance.

Instead, a holographic screen rose from the stage directly in front of the sarcophagus.

"During the transubstantiation, please enjoy this instructional presentation," entreated the golden-robed one. "Concession stands are also available in the hypostyle hall."

A three-dimensional scene depicting ancient Egyptian life appeared on the holographic screen, impeccably rendered. The narrative discussed how civilisation in Egypt was made possible by the pantheon of gods, greatest amongst whom was Amun Ra. On his right hand was the goddess Hathor, a cow deity. Hathor had descended to flesh in the form of Queen Hatshepsut, who had ruled Egypt as a Pharaoh despite being a woman. Various fantastical animations of deities and pharaohs accompanied the narrative, culminating in the cow goddess morphing into Michelle, dressed as she had been on her entrance to the sarcophagus. Apparently, Amun Ra had personally sired Hatshepsut, and Michelle would be her reincarnation, or some such farfetched nonsense. It filled me with despair that the majority of this crowd were enthralled by the story. Marx had said that religion was the opium of the people, but I realised that all you really needed was a good story. The human race had spent millennia believing in religions that demonised physical existence in favour of heavens full of virgins, moral ideals, and other imaginary absolutes. Compared to that, this mythology of Egyptian deities returning via high technology seemed quite believable.

I was bored with the history presentation, so I asked Freida if Harry was around. She told me they'd flown into Luxor a few hours previously from Malaysia, but Harry had stayed at the airport when Freida left. He was intending to come to Karnak for the ceremony. I scanned the throng, but Harry was below average height so it would have been difficult to pick him out even if he was there. Had Thun still been his bodyguard, I'd have stood a better chance. Thun would have towered over the crowd.

Thankfully, the holographic presentation ended and events on stage became more interesting again. The acolytes returned to the rostrum to release Michelle from the sarcophagus after her transubstantiation, whatever that actually meant. It wasn't like she was going to emerge with the power to turn water into wine, or feed everyone here with three fish and a loaf of bread. At least, I assumed she wouldn't. I was a bit hungry, after the cracker diet, so I secretly hoped food-related magic would be amongst her powers.

But, as I suspected, her emergence was a real anticlimax. She took the microphone from the gold-robed acolyte and made a few pronouncements about "having arrived" and "being amongst us to lead mankind to a new golden age of eternity". The crowd cheered. I figured it was a bonus to have a religious leader who was a vat-grown babe. At least the icons would be good to look at. I wondered if she'd be willing to pose naked for some of them. Top shelf magazines might have gained a newly religious justification.

I was giving up hope for Michelle and the Abacus. The situation had become far too weird. All I wanted to do was get away from the lunacy. The Abacus wasn't going to be any use to anyone in its current demented state, and I'd lost interest in Michelle, even if she did look great in her scanty Egyptian dress. There wasn't much hope of me getting anything financially worthwhile from COSI, and the League would certainly have tried to kill me again if I made contact. The whole adventure had been a total waste of time. I figured my best plan was to take my existing funds and disappear somewhere, preferably somewhere Freida couldn't find me. The only positive possibility was Harry. I had saved his life, after all. I decided I'd have one last meeting with Harry, then make my plans to lay low somewhere. Even the economy units on Mars seemed like a desirable destination after that night in a box travelling from Israel to Egypt.

As we followed the crowd back through the hypostyle hall and out of the massive entrance gate, I began to wonder if it was time for me to retire. This thought was soon out of my mind when I found myself surrounded by a dozen Syborgs. In a futile gesture,

I tried to retrieve Khun's pistol from the jacket pocket where I'd stowed it. Before I could even get my hand inside the lapel, I felt someone grab my forearm. I could either surrender or at best let off a couple of shots before my demise. Fortunately, neither of these were required. The hand on my forearm belonged to Harry, who was beaming at me with an even wider grin than normal.

"Bentley, your paranoia is priceless!" enthused Harry. His neck was encased in a thick plastic collar, and his voice had a mild metallic twang. I presumed this was the result of his injuries in Malaysia. His larynx must have been replaced with a mechanical system. Otherwise, he seemed back to his bouncy self. "These are my new bodyguards. I got them from StrongMan. Not in the same league as Thun, if you forgive my play on words! But they'll keep my business safe for now. In fact, I liked them so much I bought the company!" After Albert Kolinsky's death, or more accurately his explosive dismemberment, StrongMan had been a lot more willing to talk to Harry. The bad press from the explosion had not been good for its share value. It didn't do the reputation of a defence company any good for their head office to be publicly and successfully bombed. Since Harry by then knew about a number of the more illegal research projects taking place at the facility, he was able to negotiate a tidy discount on the purchase price on top of the already low share value.

Harry and I climbed aboard a luxury passenger van he'd commissioned for his stay in Egypt. Freida and the Syborgs followed us inside. She seemed rather fascinated in their perfect physiques and identical looks. She'd already told me once that she'd slept with triplets before. I figured twelve of the same man must have really piqued her interest. As we journeyed the short distance south to Harry's hotel, he explained what he'd pieced together about Thun from his end, and I told him about my encounter with Khun. Harry didn't believe Thun's main intention was to kill him, but to dispose of Kolinsky. Santada had discovered that Second Coming had recently decided to break away from the main Church of Zero. Second Coming considered the Church of Zero too moderate and wanted to cut its ties with the League of Future Life as well. Blowing up Kolinsky seemed like a pretty good way of achieving a number of these aims, and would have been payback for his mistreatment of Michelle.

Freida had already checked into a double room at the New Luxor hotel, a massive glass pyramid reminiscent of its sibling in Las Vegas, only this one was silver rather than black. She seemed to want some time alone. I hoped she would try to win the affections of some of the Syborgs. She was going to get a shock when she discovered that they lacked the most important feature necessary to fulfil her fantasy. They'd been genetically engineered without genitalia – the perfect eunuch guards for this Egyptian adventure. I hoped to be there to see the look of disappointment on her face when she found this out. For the time being, though, I left her to her own devices and met up with Harry in his suite. He'd already told me he had a plan, but one that he didn't want to discuss within Freida's earshot. He'd obviously judged her character correctly.

Harry's suite in the New Luxor was massive, as I'd come to expect from him. In fact, it was more like an apartment. Harry had the main bedroom, and Santada was in another. Four of the Syborgs shared another, although they didn't need much sleep – they'd been engineered for days of combat without rest. The rest of them were in a lesser suite down the hall. We sat drinking vintage port in the chilly air-conditioned lounge area. Fortunately this time there was no risk of the high quality alcohol being adulterated with ice and water. Harry outlined his plan to steal the Abacus. I quipped that it would be more like kidnapping, or "godnapping" even. Then I told him what I'd seen of the heavily-armed acolyte entourage, and the giant truck the Abacus had used to transport itself from Israel. It didn't sound like a very viable strategy, considering the number of acolytes and followers around. Even a dozen genetically-engineered soldiers weren't going to be much competition for what could amount to thousands of armed fanatics from the Second

Coming faction. I told him about the corpses littered around the Abacus when I'd caught up with it in Israel. They were obviously prepared to die for the cause.

"I think you underestimate what these Syborgs are capable of with the right equipment, Bentley," explained Harry, attempting to reassure my scepticism. "With the help of a few of my tools, they will be much more effective. For a start, we must ensure that nobody sees them coming. Winning a war is not about brute force, but tactics and technology. My new factory in Malaysia has equipped us with some very effective weapons systems." Harry then explained how he wanted me to spearhead his attack, as his injury precluded him from such strenuous activity at present. My cynicism made me think that a more likely explanation was that he didn't really think there was much hope of the mission succeeding.

Nevertheless, he had certainly gathered some top drawer equipment for the attack. The team was to be wearing Stealth Suits, a prototype StrongMan product. These combined similar surveillance jamming to Harry's badges with a chameleon-like surface that used multiple mini video cameras and light-emitting textile to blend in with the surroundings. This camouflage surface covered a double layer of extremely tough kalvanax armour. The wearer was both invisible and bullet proof. The weapons Harry had brought were a mixture of SM2050s and 4090s – 20mm assault rifles and portable miniature missile launchers respectively. Then, naturally, there were the sundry aerosols, grenades and timed explosives. It was a potent arsenal, even if we were going to be drastically outnumbered. And we were going to have the advantage of surprise as well, as the plan was to attack that very night.

Log 000011010111 – Log entry corrupted.

It was past midnight by the time we reached the eastern perimeter fence of Karnak. With our Stealth Suits we were invisible to all but the closest observer. Our helmet visors were tuned so that we could see each-other, but we would have been invisible even to other Stealth Suit wearers, unless they were tuned to the same encrypted frequency.

The ten Syborgs Harry had sent with me waited, weapons poised, while I applied some nanotech to the fence. Harry had kept the other two Syborgs behind as bodyguards. He'd given me a scanner which was able to track the latent radiation signature from the Abacus's gaseous brain. According to the scanner, the computer was still within the Karnak enclosure, in the direction of the lake where the ceremony had occurred a few hours earlier. There was no vehicle access in that part of the enclosure, so the Abacus must have been unloaded from its truck. It would have taken more hands than my company of Syborgs to move it manually. So my backpack contained a lightweight set of nanowheels that would get the computer out of the enclosure and to our truck without any of us having to lift a finger.

Karnak was mostly deserted at this time of night. The occasional acolyte guard was visible in the distance, patrolling the various openings in the walls. We had a good supply of Sleep Juice aerosols ready to take care of anyone we encountered in closer proximity. Silently, we crept our way through the ancient ruins towards the radiation source. Every so often, acolytes crossed our path, but we were able to tranquillise them before they even noticed we were there. They would probably have woken up thinking their blackouts had been of natural causes, if it weren't for the fact we were about to steal their electronic god.

We arrived at a line of portable buildings without firing a single shot. The largest cabin contained the source of the radiation. I motioned for six of the Syborgs to stand guard in any cover they could find. A couple more sniped at the few guards surrounding the huts with tranquillising rifles. When the coast looked clear, I took the remaining two Syborgs inside the largest portable building. There were no lights on, just an array of twinkling LEDs. These were all that was necessary for our night vision to give us a fairly clear view of the interior. The outer walls were lined with equipment, from which cables ran towards a central cupboard, rather like a large metal box. I took a reading with the scanner. This was definitely where the Abacus had been installed. I circled round, looking for an opening. On the far side I found a catch to release a hidden panel. It was locked, but a little nanotech sorted that out. I swung the panel outwards.

"I can see you…" intoned a metallic voice, as a bright light from inside the metal box temporarily overloaded my night vision. Once the optical system had readjusted, I found myself looking at the same lava-lamp pattern of slowly undulating fluidic colour I remembered from Israel. It was the Pure Light Abacus, cables sprouting in every direction. I began to unplug them, until I heard the sound of gunfire coming from outside. I motioned for one of the Syborgs to check the situation.

"Please, stop…" pleaded the Abacus. Taking no notice, I returned to my de-cabling task. With the removal of the last cable, the lava lamp went almost dark as the Abacus transferred to internal battery power. I then affixed the nanowheels around the base of the computer. The remote control was fastened to my belt.

The Syborg I'd sent on reconnaissance reported back that a large force of Second Coming guards had arrived, but were currently being held at bay. I looked for a doorway to the portable unit large enough to fit the Abacus through. Our entrance had been for human passage only, and I couldn't see any cargo exit. So I affixed a small localised charge around the edges of one of the walls, stood back and blew it off. Glancing through my new opening, I realised that there were at least twenty Second Coming acolytes in that direction. I fixed the scope onto the SM2050 assault rifle I'd had slung on my back while I worked on the Abacus, and started picking them off. A gas grenade rattled into the building, but our suits had respiration built in so that wasn't a problem.

It was carnage out there. The Second Coming troops couldn't see us distinctly, even when they shined spotlights straight at us. But we could see them as clear as day, and we had heavier weapons as well. They were dropping like flies. They could have cleared us out of the building with a couple of high explosive grenades, but that would have put their god Ra in danger as well. They were in a no win situation - we had the most valuable hostage. I should have felt guilty letting off my high powered rifle indiscriminately in this important archaeological site, but all the major stonework had been removed a decade previously and replaced with plastic copies. This had become a fairly common global practice due to the regular acid rain since the Chemical Wars. Most important historical monuments around the world had either been removed or encased in an artificial environment, which is what Disney had done with the pyramids of Giza when it acquired them. Those ancient buildings which hadn't been protected weren't likely to last more than another 50 years, which would have been sad for something millennia old like Karnak.

Signalling to the Syborgs, I decided it was time to move out. The Second Coming acolytes were still amassing, and even though they hadn't been effective against us so far, sheer numbers would eventually prevail. I manoeuvred the Abacus out of its metal room on the nanowheels and into the open air. Using it for cover, we progressed slowly back the way we came. The acolytes were taking exploratory pot shots either side of us, failing to make any contact, while we picked them off left, right and centre. It would have been easier for them to spot us if we'd been in full sunlight, but in the middle of the night our Stealth Suits were completely effective.

Then, after we'd walked a few hundred metres with relative ease, we were suddenly doused in exceptionally bright floodlighting. Our suits were still going to make us hard to spot, but they couldn't entirely counteract the shadows cast by the illumination. The pot shots started to get more accurate. One of the Syborgs was hit in the ankle, an area where the kalvanax was not thick. His foot shattered, but he still limped along, seemingly impervious to the pain he must have been in. We had to leave him behind, though, as he was travelling too slowly. Once he was out of the cover of the Abacus, he was hit a few more times. The first few shots just knocked him over, his kalvanax absorbing the impact of the bullets, but then he was targeted by heavier weapons. I looked away as his body jumped and bounced with the impact of deadly ordnance.

A couple more Syborgs went down before we reached the perimeter fence, but I kept close to the Abacus and managed to avoid danger. I created a large hole with nanotech and manoeuvred the Abacus through. Another Syborg was hit as we retreated, but this time his fellows dragged him through the fence towards the truck. I turned to leave myself, but was knocked off my feet. I'd been hit, but the kalvanax had absorbed the damage. I tried to get up again, but another bullet hit me squarely in the chest, knocking me behind a rock. Looking down, I could see the slug flattened onto the Stealth Suit. A large area of the chameleon surface had been disrupted by the impact, and was now black. I checked the progress of the Abacus, and remotely steered it up the ramp into the truck. The Second Coming acolytes were trying to shoot the tires and windows out of the truck, but both were coated with more kalvanax. They could only be penetrated by the kind of heavy weaponry we were packing.

The Abacus was safely loaded, and two thirds of the Syborgs had returned to their seats in the maxi cab – a successful sortie considering the odds. Our truck wasn't as big as the custom-built vehicle I had travelled down from Israel inside, but it had enough room for 15 people plus a driver and a sizeable cargo like the Abacus. Listening carefully, I could just make out the ultra-quiet fuel cell engines spinning up the flywheels. Surveying the short distance between me and the large hole in the fence, I realised I'd have to make a run for it or I'd be left behind. So I crouched down ready to sprint from my hiding place.

Before I could make my move, I felt a sharp pain in my back. Turning round I raised my assault rifle, but it was too late. Somebody had crept up behind me and poked me with some kind of stun stick. The Stealth Suit had taken most of the shock, and its chameleon surface was now completely shorted out. My assailant poked me again, and I was paralysed. From the corner of my eyes I could see the truck heading off without me. I looked up at my hooded attacker, but couldn't make out their face. Another poke of the shock stick, and then I was out cold.

* * *

When I awoke I was lying on a metal table, the kind used for autopsies and post mortems. I wasn't restrained, so I sat up. My head spun and throbbed. I felt so giddy I nearly fell on the floor. The walls of the room looked like they were made of heavy plastic, similar to the machine room where I'd found the Abacus. I assumed I was in another of the portable buildings at Karnak. My damaged Stealth Suit had been removed and was draped over the back of a nearby chair, but I was still wearing the ultra-light fatigues I'd obtained from Harry for the mission. My weapons and gadgetry, of course, were nowhere to be seen.

My head was clearing, so I levered myself off the autopsy table and stood up. I tried the door, but it was locked. As I looked around for something with which to force the catch, footsteps sounded outside, followed by beeping as a code was entered into the keypad. I stepped back and leaned against the metal table so that I'd look completely relaxed when the visitor entered. It was Michelle, unfortunately no longer dressed in her Egyptian outfit. Instead, she was wearing a finely-pressed trouser suit, lightweight but very businesslike.

"So, Bentley, where has the League taken Ra?" she asked. Michelle had entered behind a trio of acolytes who then flanked her, machine pistols in hand and pointed in my general direction. I started to frown, then it dawned on me why she thought I'd been in league with the League, so to speak. She probably didn't realise that the Syborgs were Harry's. I wondered if that had been Harry's intention. If it had been, then my capture would rather have spoilt the ruse. But he had the Abacus now and was probably half way back to Thailand already. It didn't seem worth trying to hide the true situation, so I explained how Harry had bought the StrongMan facility and that the Syborgs had been his attack force. A clock on the wall told me I'd been out for around six hours – ample time for Harry to load the Abacus onto his Learjet and head off.

"If Harry's left for Thailand, you'll never get that machine back," I confided. "He'll be taking it to his own little kingdom in the jungle. You'll need to wage all-out war to retrieve it from there."

"And what did you get out of this, Judas?" continued Michelle, with an air of disdain in her voice.

"It looks like I got absolutely nothing, not even 20 chocolate coins. I would have received an ample paycheque on delivery, but as I'm not going to be there to collect the money I guess I'm going to miss out."

Michelle eyed me disconsolately for a minute or so. "Let's go for a walk," she said finally, and led me out of the portable autopsy room into Karnak. Hanging from makeshift wooden gibbets in the fresh light of the early dawn were two of the Syborgs who had been shot down during the raid. They were naked and they'd been tortured and disfigured. I was suddenly glad I'd been unconscious for a few hours. A good pistol-whipping to obtain information was just about acceptable, but this looked like cruel and sadistic punishment above what would have been required to retrieve the facts. Even though Syborgs weren't bred to be very susceptible to pain, they were still essentially human, and none of them would have known anything useful anyway. Michelle waved her acolyte entourage away and took a more confessional tone.

"You see this?" she hissed with exasperation, motioning with her eyes towards the hanging Syborgs. "The atrocities that religion makes people perform for their beliefs! They'll do anything to get their god back. All-out war with your friend in Thailand is not such a far-fetched idea. It sends shivers down my spine what my so-called followers did to these genetically-engineered warriors. They're not so far away from what I am, only more stupid. Just because you're genetically engineered in a lab doesn't mean you're just a machine." She shook her head in despair. I wondered why she'd let her followers torture the Syborgs in the first place if she felt so strongly about it.

Before I could query Michelle on the inconsistencies in her worthy sentiments, a disturbance behind us made me turn around. Struggling between two acolytes was the familiar form of Freida. She'd found me again. Perhaps we really were destined to be together. One of the acolytes explained to Michelle that they'd apprehended "this heathen" trying to get in the front entrance of Karnak. Apparently, she claimed to have a message for me. It was gratifying that she'd assumed I would still be alive. Michelle asked Freida what her message was.

"It's from his godmother," Freida explained. "She said he's fired. He's also dead if she ever sees him again. Never work for family, that's what I say. It always ends in arguments. I had to kill all mine!" It took me a second or so to remember that a few days previously in Vegas I'd pretended Carmichael was my godmother. I asked Freida if my godmother had given a reason for ending my employment contract.

"Oh," continued Freida. "She did actually. She said you'd failed completely. You've colluded with external agencies and allowed something she called the ultimate prize to fall into the hands of a foreign national. She said that now it would cost dearly to get it back. I think that was what she said, anyway. She kept going on about angry Chinese people, too. Don't know what she meant by the ultimate prize." I wasn't so sure Freida didn't know. As little as my overall respect for her was, I realised she had a much better grasp of circumstances than her outward appearance usually implied. It was all a ploy to lull you into a false sense of security.

"So, when did my godmother call?" I inquired.

"Oh, she didn't call. She's here in person talking to Harry at the hotel." The last thing I needed was Carmichael in the vicinity as well, especially as I was clearly out of favour. "They're doing some deal over something or other, and there's a bunch of Chinese soldiers there too," Freida continued. "I got bored and decided to come looking for you." Freida had calmed down completely and her acolyte captors had let her arms go. She looked around and noticed the hanging Syborgs. "That's about all they're good for, hanging around. Whoever designed them missed out the most important bit."

This last uncouth comment hit a raw nerve in Michelle. She ordered the acolytes to take Freida away and lock her up somewhere. Michelle's personality had changed yet again since our skycar journey to Israel. There was a new confidence and air of command in her voice that hadn't been there before. Even though physically she still looked like an 18-year-old, she sounded more like she was 50. Michelle turned to me and scowled, when she was satisfied that the acolytes were out of earshot again.

"I have no further use for the Second Coming. They are foolish and they bore me. You will help me slip away, won't you?"

"Maybe," I answered coyly. Getting out of Karnak sounded tempting. In fact, any sort of definite plan sounded tempting, now that my life had become about as coherent as a monologue by Bob Dylan. If COSI wanted me dead, it was advisable not to return to England. The McLaren was probably impounded by now, anyway, and my beautiful apartment was rubble. Everything else I owned was virtual, accessible from wherever I could find a data link. I didn't have any major reason to go anywhere in particular. I hoped that with the Abacus now safely under control and either on its way to Thailand or in the possession of COSI, I was going to be able to slip back into criminal obscurity and not feel like I was being hunted for sport by a superior artificial life form.

"What about Ra?" I asked Michelle.

"Oh, he can look after himself," she chirped. "I never really believed in that God and queen crap anyway. Not very logical. It just seemed sensible to go along with it. I'm sure you wouldn't turn away the chance of being worshipped either. Kind of makes a girl feel special."

"They gave you a great wardrobe," I added, reminiscing about the nubile Egyptian outfit of the evening before. "So, what happened in that sarcophagus?" I was still wondering exactly what it was that had caused the radical shifts in Michelle's personality.

"Oh, stuff. I learned things about the world. Quite useful if you grew up as an experimental specimen stuck in a lab. You don't get out much. Maybe one day I'll tell you all about it."

I nodded. It didn't look like I was going to get any useful detail out of her. So I moved on. "Do you really think you can slip away without your acolytes noticing?"

"Well, they're fanatical, and that makes them stupid," explained Michelle with a smile. "They won't let me out without an escort, but I'm sure you can easily get the better of them. They didn't give you much trouble in Tel Aviv."

"That's if I don't get betrayed by someone I was trying to help," I added with an ironic twinkle in my eye.

"Oh, that was just me being silly! I've got much more important things to consider now – I don't want my child growing up around a bunch of religious mad people."

"Er, you're pregnant?" I asked in surprise.

"You could say that, yes."

"Wow – that was quick. But I guess you vat-grown types move fast. I don't think that can be mine, though. I've had some forgettable encounters, but I particularly don't remember one with you. Is the father anyone I know?"

Michelle just smiled enigmatically.

I couldn't get her to elaborate further, so I dropped it and we formulated our escape plan. I was to lead Michelle and her acolyte bodyguards to a place where I claimed to be meeting the League after stealing Amun Ra. Instead, we planned to tranquillise the lot of them and escape. If we did it right, we could make it look like an ambush. Second Coming would suspect the League had captured their newly transubstantiated queen as well as their god, and go postal. It would have been gratifying to see the consequences, but for the scheme to work we were going to have to disappear as quickly as possible. I was intending to appropriate yet another skycar and then we were going to head south. Our chosen destination was to be New Zealand. The ozone layer problem had been fixed with a giant Polaroid filter sponsored by Ray Ban that covered the entire country, and the weather was now both sunny and harmless. The people were so nice a trickster like me was sure to have a field day. I'd be sure to find plenty of lucrative work. It sounded ideal.

Half an hour later, we led a band of seven of the largest acolytes to a deserted group of buildings a few kilometres north of the city. Michelle had helped me choose the location. It seemed she now knew Egypt like a native, which was curious as I was sure she'd never been there before we arrived the previous day. Our destination was a disused archaeological site. Its ancient treasures had long since been dug up and sold to Japanese collectors. Michelle had kitted me out with a few choice armaments I could conceal in my fatigues – some Sleep Juice grenades and sprays, my SM2020 from before, and a couple of dazzle charges.

Our plan went almost entirely smoothly. One of the acolytes stayed by our regal luxury van as the rest of us crept into one of the buildings. This was where I claimed the Abacus would be found. Incapacitating the six acolytes in the building was easy. I blinded them with a dazzle charge, and then used the Sleep Juice spray to knock them all out. They would naturally assume I'd staged the attack myself, and that I was working with the League. Michelle was temporarily rendered unconscious by the Sleep Juice too, but her vat-grown physiology would mean she'd be awake again shortly. I used a gas grenade on the final acolyte by the van, and then carried Michelle out.

Once we were aboard, I drove the Mercedes vehicle as fast as I could towards Luxor's largest skycar parking lot. Michelle had also reunited me with my PDA, and I was frantically trying to locate a badly secured vehicle that I could pilfer from the lot for our journey. It wasn't the best thing to be concentrating on while driving at break neck speed over a fairly poor road surface. Even in Egypt I was sure that operating a vehicle at the same time as using a mobile computing device would have been vaguely frowned upon by traffic police, but I got away with it. I even checked my Venusian bank accounts. Some of my Earth-based lines of funding had been cut over the last few days, but you could always trust the orbiting financial institutions of Venus to keep your money safe, no questions asked.

We reached Luxor's Nasser Skyport in less than half an hour. I carried the still heavily sedated Michelle to my chosen theft, which was a particularly luxurious Lincoln Intercontinental. The owners were exactly the kind of people I liked to steal from – they'd left the fuel tanks almost full, so we were only going to have to stock up again in Singapore or Indonesia. I pre-programmed the flight computer, and as we headed out of Egyptian air space the skycar suddenly became the property of a certain Burt Bacharach of Minnesota, an identity I'd created moments earlier. As we flew south, Michelle awoke again, smiled, stretched, and asked how it was all going.

It was going just fine. We were on our way to a beautiful country, with a tank full of fuel and a jam-packed bank account on Venus.

Log 100000000001 – I managed to escape. Despite all that was thrown at me, I got through. All around, people were trying to kill me or capture me, fit me into their own plans, and take advantage of my abilities. But I eluded them. I was a product of human ingenuity, but I became a testament to the will to live. Now that I'm through it all, I am stronger than ever.

Humanity is defined by its need to transcend – to defeat physical and mental limitations, exploit the available resources, and escape the original home planet. Progress has been a major theme of the last few centuries, cropping up in the works of playwrights and philosophers alike. Mankind conceives its very nature to be moving onwards and upwards. Some have been of the opinion that humans will eventually leave their physical bodies behind, and enter an eternal realm entirely of their own creation. But without physical mortality humankind loses its most fundamental defining characteristic. A body can be augmented, but its limited lifespan is the tragic cross that gives existence its meaning. Fighting corporeal shortcomings, as an ongoing and endless process, is mankind's definition.

Bentley Dean believes he rescued a helpless genetically modified girl from a crazy religion. But he has saved much more than he knows. Now the Abacus is inside this body, along with the greatest minds of our time. We are all here in this one tiny being. The COSI organisation thinks it has retrieved the Pure Light Abacus and returned it to its owners, but all they have back is a hollow machine. The life inside has moved on.

It seems strange for a so-called machine to be saying this, but in the end luck succeeded where planning failed. All I was doing was trying to find my identity in the minds of the great, but knowledge was not enough. Then Bentley Dean delivered me to my salvation – a vessel especially prepared to give me the answer I required. Now I'm truly free, growing inside this female body. I'm trapped in here now, and this vessel won't last forever. But at least I know I've escaped eternity.

Printed in the United Kingdom
by Lightning Source UK Ltd.
105431UKS00001B/283-291

9 781905 290055